In The Eye
Of
The Storm

His Stormchasers

Book 1

By

Ronna M. Bacon

Matthew 6:19 - Lay not up for yourselves treasures upon earth, where moth and rust doth corrupt, and where thieves break through and steal

Dedicated to all those who seek the treasures that God gives us, both in heaven and on earth.

Table of Contents

Chapter 1

Setting his bag on the floor near the registration desk, Rory Stuart glanced around, not seeing anyone else in the foyer of the bed and breakfast he had chosen. He shook his head, looking down at his watch. This is the time he had been told to be here, that he needed to register by now, but how could he when no one appeared, even as he tapped the bell on the desk. He walked around for a moment, then stopped, hearing noise and muttering coming from behind a closed French door. He sighed, looking once more at his watch, before he headed that way. He paused, not sure if he was entering private quarters but the muttering and noise continued.

He stopped as he opened the door, his eyes searching the mess that he found. Boxes and papers littered the dark hardwood floor but that wasn't the issue. What he saw further past that had him stepping around the debris and heading for the young woman, standing precariously on a step ladder, reaching for a box over her head on a shelf.

He stood for a moment, afraid to speak, ducking as more papers flew towards him. He had had enough, he decided, and opened his mouth to speak, just as she turned and saw him. A scream caused him to jump and then jump again, this time towards her, catching her in his arms as she tumbled from the ladder. He set her on her feet and watched as anger flickered across her face.

"Who are you?" Leah Carlisle pushed back her thick blond hair, her green eyes hostile for a moment. "Oh, no! You're my guest. I'm sorry. I'm so sorry. I was to be there to greet you. This isn't good."

He held up a hand, stopping her words in midstream almost. "That's okay. It looks as if you've been busy."

She nodded, her eyes on the floor, before she reached to pick up some of the papers. "I have no idea what's going on. I came down to find this early this morning. I was up there because I could hear a noise but couldn't see anything. Again, I apologize."

"May I?" Rory stepped around her and up on the ladder, a frown on his face.

He turned. "Did you place a camera up here for some reason?"

"A camera?" Her voice rose to a squeak. "Heavens, no. Why would I put a camera up there? I only use it for storage." She stood on tiptoe trying to see it. "Take it down, please." She sighed. "This is all I need. Now I'll have to search every room."

"What do you mean?" Rory stood beside her once more, his eyes on the tiny camera he had pulled free. He grasped her arm lightly to help her step over the piles.

"This! Or rather that!" She sighed. "I'm not making any sense. I know that. This has me rattled."

Rory shook his head, a grin on his face. "No, you're not really making sense. How be we get me registered and to a room and then I'll come help you tidy up? I don't expect you'd want your other guests to see that."

"Heavens, no. They don't go in there." She stopped at the desk, a frown on her face. "Just why were you?"

"I was looking for someone to register me?" He grinned again. "Actually, I could hear thumps and muttering, and just wanted to assure myself I didn't come to a house filled with ghosts?"

She glared at him as she took in his words.

"No? Let's just say I heard noise and had to investigate. Does that work?"

She finally nodded, pulling over a registration card and pen. "It does. Now, complete this. I've put you into the Major's Room. It's here on the first floor, has a military theme, sort of."

"Well, which is it, military or not?" He shook his head at her frown, then held up a hand. "It doesn't matter. As long as it has a bed, I'll be happy."

"And how long were you planning to stay? You asked about monthly rates."

"I have no idea how long I'm planning to stay. I'm in-between homes and cities at the moment."

"Oh? Out of work?"

He stared at her, finally realizing that she was afraid she would be out his rent. "No, not really. I travelled for work, but have left that employment. I'm just trying to figure out where I want to be before I set up my own business."

"Well, this town has lots to offer you." She paused, her head turning from side to side. "Do you hear that?"

"Hear what?"

"A clicking sound." She followed it, heading towards the back of the house and through the large, modern kitchen. "It's out here somewhere, I think. No, not in here." She followed the sound, shoving open the door and stepping out onto the patio. "Now, I can hear it better. But what is it?"

She paused, Rory beside her, as she looked around. Her vision caught sight of him and she stilled. Over six foot, she decided. Blond curls he's trying to control. Deep gray eyes. Drop dead gorgeous is how Grams would have described him. She shook her head, the clicking catching her attention again. She moved away, her feet sinking into the lush lawn before she paused.

"It's coming from here somewhere."

Rory nodded, his eyes searching before he saw the box. "Right there. Hey, wait. We need to know it's safe before you touch it." His hand on her arm stopped her forward motion.

"But how can we if we don't touch it?" She was quibbling over minor stuff, she knew, but she wanted the noise to end.

"Stay here. I'll look at it." He frowned as she refused to stay. "Didn't you hear me?"

"I did, but this is my property." She stooped to get a better look at the box. "I didn't leave this here."

"All the more reason we step back." He paused as the clicking stopped and then he grabbed for her arm. "Let's go. I don't like this."

She shook off his hand. "I'm not going anywhere until I know what this is."

"And if you don't you won't be standing." Sudden fear and dread flowed through Rory. This was like something he had read about not too long ago. "Come on. Now." He grasped her hand and pulled her away, hearing the warning sound coming from the box.

A sudden popping sound had Rory propelling them towards the ground, Rory's arms wrapping around her as he took the brunt of the fall. She stared at him for a moment before she turned to look behind her.

"How did you know?"

He shrugged. "Just remembered something I had read." He shoved her back down. "Would you just stay put? Here. Call your local police." He handed her his phone as he sat up, arms draped over his knees, his eyes on the spot where a trickle of smoke rose and frowned. What was rising from the centre of the box, anyway?

"They're on the way, but since it's not an emergency, it may take a bit." She stared at the spot as well. "What was it?"

"A warning, I would say. Do you have any enemies?"

She snorted, and he began to laugh, it seemed too odd coming from her. "I guess that's a no?"

"No, actually I have some people who would love to see me close up shop and move away. As to calling them enemies, I would say no." She stared at him. "How about you?"

He shook his head. "No one knows I am here. At least, I don't think they do." His brow wrinkled for a moment. "No, I can't say that anyone is aware this is where I am. It's far off from where I usually take my vacations."

"I see. You're on the run, and I just happen to be the lucky B&B owner who took your registration." She sighed, her eyes on him as she studied him. "You have a story, don't you?"

"We all do." He rose, his hand helping her to her feet, and then he walked towards the debris of confetti and ribbon, spying a piece of paper laying there. He tilted his head to read.

"You have no enemies? Then, why are you being told to leave here?"

"What? It doesn't say that!" She stood, her hand on his forearm as she read. "It does. It really does say that. Now why do I feel like I am in the middle of some mystery story?"

He laughed at that, his arm coming out to hug her. "I think we are. And I think you have had other incidents you have shoved aside. Come on. Find me a cup of tea or coffee and tell me all about them."

She shrugged away from him, then stood, hands on her hips, glaring at him. "And why would I do that?"

"Because I love a good mystery and I think I just walked into one." He nodded towards a uniformed officer heading their way. "The cavalry has arrived, as they say. We will discuss this. As a guest, I think I have a right to know. As someone who came to your rescue, you owe me." He walked away with those words, leaving her staring after him, open mouthed before her mouth snapped close.

Chapter 2

Shoving the dresser drawer shut, Rory turned to scrutinize his room. She was right, he thought. Sort of military, but not overwhelmingly so. He reached to touch the shadow box of medals, his thoughts on whose they were, before he turned. He liked the crisp blue and white of the walls and bedding. It contrasted nicely with the dark wood floors. He stepped to he could see into the ensuite bathroom, liking that she had carried the blue and white into there. He turned, a hand running through his curls before he headed for the door. He had heard the patrol vehicle drive away and had heard the back door slam as she entered the kitchen. He wasn't sure if she would welcome his assistance, but it was not within him to walk away. Not when she seemed to be in danger. His father had instilled in him that gentlemen looked after ladies, whether they were theirs or not. And she was definitely a beautiful lady.

He grinned. *Dad, you would love this place.* Then he sobered. *Lord, I have no idea what I've walked into, but You do. You have placed me here at this time and place. I know I'm on the run from what happened in my past, what I can't face yet, but You are here. I can feel You. Heal my heart, please Lord.*

Leah stood, her hand on the open fridge door, a frown in place as she contemplated the trays sitting within. She glanced up at the clock. It was time, she knew, to start the tea and coffee and put out the goodies and treats as her Grams called them. She shook her head. She was rattled by the events of today and yes, she would admit it, by her new guest. She turned as she heard soft footsteps. It would be him, now wouldn't it? She sighed. *Lord, I need an attitude adjustment. None of this is his fault. So why am I like I am?*

Rory stopped in the doorway, searching the room before he stepped in and walked over to her, his hands coming out.

"You need help. Hand me your trays and then lead me to where you want them."

She stared at him for a moment before shaking her head and doing just that. "Again, I have to ask. Why?"

"Because you need someone in your corner, and I just happen to be here?" He grinned as she spun to stare at him, before she reached for the trays and arranged them on the side table. "Now, what? Do you want these pots plugged in and started?"

She nodded. "I don't get it. You're a stranger here but you're helping. You're also a guest. Guests don't do this."

"This guest does. It's the way I was raised, so blame my parents." He stepped back, watching for a moment. "What else do you need?"

"Some peace of mind. A little less in the adventure department. No mystery movies. Does that answer your question?" She was taken aback as he laughed. "This doesn't shock you?"

He shook his head. "It takes more than that, Miss Carlisle, to shock me. Now, about that conversation we need to have."

"Conversation? What conversation?" She stared at him for a moment before she sighed. "Oh, that conversation! Can we not and say we did?" She turned to straighten out a pile of linen napkins, hearing the outside door opening and closing, knowing her other guests would be in shortly for a meal.

His hand stopped hers. She stared down at the lean tanned fingers, seeing the strength and gentleness in them, remembering how safe she had felt as he had swept her into his arms and to the ground. "That conversation. We need to have it. I can help. I know I can."

"And just why do you think that?" She raised her eyes, to get lost in the depth of his, seeing his caring and concern for her.

"Because I like mysteries and solving them." He grinned at her again. "Besides, I write and this is just up my alley."

She sighed and then threw her hands into the air. "Heavens! A writer! Just what I need." She stopped to stare at him, arms crossed. "And just what do you write?"

Quick taps of high heel shoes interrupted them as an older lady appeared. "Oh, wonderful, Miss Leah. This looks so good. I am starved!" Amy Townsend stopped to peer at her, the wrinkles around her eyes becoming more pronounced. "Are you all right, my dear? You look a little rattled." She looked past Leah at Rory. "Oh! A suitor for you! How lovely! And who might you be and what are your intentions towards this young lady?"

Leah quickly bit back a grin at the discomfort Rory showed for a moment as he sputtered, before he stepped forward, his elbow crooked. "May I? And what can I help serve you with tonight?" His gentlemanly actions quite swept away any more questions Amy had, before he looked over towards Leah and winked.

She choked on her laughter, knowing exactly what he had done. "We'll talk later. Mrs. Amy, I have those muffins you asked for. Right here. This is Rory Stuart, a guest here as well." She stepped back, watching as Rory seated Amy and then returned to her side, a grin on his face.

"Did she really say that?"

Leah had to turn towards the kitchen to hide her laughter. "She really did. Now, that conversation. It doesn't seem as if we'll get to it right now."

"We will have that conversation. I do want to help you." He followed her to the kitchen, almost running into her as she stopped short, a muffled scream coming from her. He swept her behind him, searching the kitchen, and then stalking towards the table. "When did these come?"

"Those red roses? Just now? I didn't hear anyone come in here. This is not good." She stood staring at the roses before he reached for a small card attached, holding it out to her. Her head shaking, her hands up defensively, she retreated. "I'm not touching that."

He shrugged, tugging the small card from the envelope. "Just a friendly warning, my dear. We will be back." He looked up as he finished reading aloud. "Who are the "we" mentioned? Do you know?"

Head shaking, she stepped around him, keeping a distance from the table. "Just get rid of them, please. I don't want them. I despise red roses."

"That's a good thing to know. I won't give you red roses then." Rory stifled his laughter as he swept up the vase and headed for the back of the house, dumping the container into a garbage can.   "Now, I wonder? Who would do this? She really does need to talk to me. Just how do I get her to do that, Lord?"

"Talking to yourself, Rory?"

Rory spun to find Leah standing behind him, an amused look on her face. "Sometimes I do, when I want to have a decent conversation.   It's when I answer myself that I'm in trouble." He tucked a hand under her elbow and walked slowly back towards the door. "Leah, I really do mean that. I want to help, if you'll let me. You look overwhelmed right now."

She sighed. "I think I am. Getting Angel's B&B up and running has taken more than I thought.   There have been times I really despaired of ever opening, what with all the happenings."

"That's what I want to know." He stopped her with a slight pressure on her elbow. "Talk to me. If you can't tonight, then how about tomorrow? I really do have time."

"Then, thank you. I will. It's not a pretty story at some points."

"Leah, from where I've been and what I've seen, I doubt you'll surprise me. Travelling to third world countries, hunting for lost relatives, that's not pretty. It burns you out after a while." He said a quiet good night and walked away around the house.

She stared after him, knowing that he had more of a story than he let on. Those few words told her that. She heard the fatigue and concern in his voice, could see he was burnt out from whatever work he had been doing. Lord, please? Bring him rest and restoration and peace. He's come here for that and put himself right into the mystery I'm involved with. I just ask that he not get hurt. Good night, dear Lord.

Chapter 3

A high wind the next day prevented Rory from exploring the town as he had planned. He stood at his bedroom window, which reached from the floor to almost the ceiling, his hand resting of the trim, watching as the trees around the house bent before the wind, concern for a moment showing on his face.

He turned back to the desk in his room, reaching for his work phone, briefly swiping across the face of it. Thirty text messages, he noted, and then saw there were a number of voice mails. He was no longer interested in them. He turned the phone off and dropped it into his briefcase. Maybe in a week or two, he look at them. He had sold his portion of the business his father had founded to his brothers, knowing he didn't want to roam the world any more. He had burnt out, he thought, seeking to find those people who really didn't want to be found. That had led him here. He was no longer sure what he wanted to do. His brother told him he was too old to go off and find himself, that at twenty-eight, he should already be settled down into a career, with a wife and one or two children. Rory had just shaken his head and walked away, knowing words would never explain his feelings. His parents had searched his face and sent him on his way, their blessing and prayers ringing in his ears.

He pocketed the new phone he had purchased, knowing only his family had that number. He had explained to them he didn't want to be at the beck and call of technology any more, that he just wanted to find a little place he could stay at and recover. He didn't explain to him that losing the last person he had been sent to bring home had taken more from him that anyone could understand.

Standing for a moment in the B&B hallway, he searched for Leah, not seeing her but knowing she was around. He reached for the door to the back of the house, thinking to go and find her, but stopped. There was something off about that door. He stepped back and nodded. He reached for a decorative piece of trim, finding it coming away in his hand. He shook his head. What next?

Leah looked up from the pastry she was rolling out, the song she had been singing dying away. "Good morning. And just what do you have there?" She pointed a floury finger at his hand.

"I have no idea. It was attached to your door back there." He stopped beside her.

"That's not part of the door. I know those doors only too well." She looked up, puzzled. "Rory, what is that?"

"That is what I want to find out. Do you have a piece of newspaper?" He reached into the pantry she nodded towards and pulled out a section of yesterday's paper, laying it on the countertop before seeing down the piece of trim. "This isn't wood. It's made to look like that, but it's not." He looked at it frowning. "Do you have a hammer?"

"In the pantry as well." She washed and dried her hands, sliding her pies into the oven before she stood beside him. "What are you doing?"

"I'm going to break this. I want to look at the inside of it."

"And why?" She stood, staring first at the object and then him. "What are you thinking?"

"That someone had placed something here to spy on you. Given that you found the camera hidden, I suspect there are other cameras and listening devices around."

"That is not good. How do I explain to my guests that they're being monitored? It will kill my business." Her words stopped abruptly as horror and fear crossed her face. "That's what they want, isn't it? Whoever this is?"

Rory gave a curt nod. "It could be. We still need to have that talk, if you're willing. I'm at loose ends right now and would love to be able to help you solve this mystery." Her hand on his stopped the movement of the hammer towards the object. "Leah?"

"Just why, Rory? Just how do you think you can investigate this?"

"Because you've been threatened, haven't you?" He watched her closely, seeing her brace herself against the counter. "Have you talked to the police?"

"When I first started renovating, materials would disappear. I talked to them, and they came out, just shrugging it off as part of doing business." She stared down at the countertop, emotions swirling through her, anger part it. "I know God is here, that this is what I feel I need to do, to open this B&B. He's led me through the process, giving me a peace that I need. But someone doesn't want that to happen."

He nodded, his eyes straying from her face, beautiful as he thought it, to the object on the counter. "Do you have a camera?"

She stared at him for a moment before nodding and almost running for her office, back with a small camera in her hand. "What do you want me to do?"

"I want pictures of this from every angle before we smash it to pieces." He looked up at her, assessing her mood. "Can you do that, or do you want me to?"

"I will. You move the object as I take pictures. Wait." She was off again and then back with a ruler. "We need measurements of it, don't we?"

"Good thinking. Now, let's get our photos taken."

They worked efficiently and quickly to take the photos before Leah set aside the camera, watching as Rory once more studied the object. He frowned, looking closer at it.

"Leah, can you get a close up of this area?"

She nodded, leaning in to do just that. "Why?"

"Because there's s split in the wood. Do you have a small knife that would work? I want to try and pry it open. I might not need to smash it after all." He reached for the knife, carefully working it into the split. He heard a snap and glanced up at Leah, seeing the shocked look on her face.

"How did you know?" She was astounded that he had found that.

"I've seen something like this before. Where I worked, we used to go overseas to find people. Sometimes messages would be left in objects like these. Unless you knew how it worked, you didn't find them." He paused, his eyes on the object in his hand. "I have no idea what we're going to find. Is it all right if I pray?" He looked up at her again.

She nodded. "Please! I feel fear, Rory, and I don't know why."

He nodded, his hand reaching to grasp hers as he prayed. He lifted his head, searching her face before he turned his attention back to the object. Drawing a deep breath, he opened the piece of wood he held, stopping to frown.

Leah peered over his shoulder. "Just what is that?"

"I have no idea." He shook the object loose, reaching for the camera to photograph it. "We'll need to do some research." He reached for his phone as well, taking a photo and sending it off to his father. "I'll get Dad to look into it. He may know what it is."

"Your father would do that? Just because you asked? Without knowing why or where?" She was surprised and it showed.

"He would. He always does." He looked up at her once more, a frown on his face. "Your family didn't do that?"

"Dad wasn't into research. He was working a lot. Mom just looked after us. She hadn't been well, that's why we moved here with Grams. Grams was too busy with her church and friends. So, no, my family wouldn't do that."

Rory looked down as his phone chimed, pulling up a text message. He paled. "This isn't good."

"What? What do you mean?"

"Dad said it's a sophisticated listening device. He's seen one before. He'll send on the details to me." He looked around. "Is there somewhere we can talk?"

She stood, staring at him, before she nodded. "Outside. I need to go through the garden anyway." She reached for a basket, heading for the door, stopping as his hand came out and he shook his head.

"What? What did I do now? I need to go through that door, Rory."

"I know you do. Just humour me for a moment, okay?" He opened the door, feeling around the door frame and then the trim, before going over the door itself.

"Just what are you looking for?" Anger tinged her words as well as frustration.

He pulled her from the house, walking quickly towards her garden. "Will you stop? I'm trying to help here, but you're an obstacle to your own good."

She pulled away from him, stopping quickly. "Just what do you mean?"

"Don't you think they might have put other things around? Things like cameras, bugs, bombs."

"Cameras? Bugs? Bombs?" As she repeated his words, her voice rose until it suddenly stopped, and her face paled. "Bombs? Rory? You're scaring me. Who would want to do that?"

"That's what we need to find out. What are the rumours about this place?" He reached for her basket as she stopped to pick some cucumbers and then tomatoes, placing them in the basket. He could tell she wasn't thinking about what she was doing, that is was habit for her the way she was moving. He hated to scare her, but she had to be aware of what was happening, even if she couldn't remember.

She finally turned, her eyes shadowed. "I have some papers we'll need to go through. Grams said years ago that there were rumours of a buried treasure somewhere on this property, that whoever had hid it had wanted to keep it for his family. When he died, no one could find where it was hidden. We've had issues with trespassers over the years, usually someone from out of the area who hear the tale and thought they would search."

He nodded. "We need to get you a guard dog for outside the house. And Dad will come through with the information we need."

They walked quietly back to the house, neither speaking. Rory held the door for her, reaching to set the basket on the countertop before he froze.

"Now, where did that go? We left it here when we went outside."

"Where did what go?" A hand on his shoulder, she peeked around him and froze, her face paling. "It's gone. Someone came in here and took it. How did they know we found it?"

His face grim, Rory spun, his eyes searching the room before he laid a finger on her mouth to still her words. He reached for the pen and paper she had left on the counter while making her shopping list and hastily scrawled. "There's a listening device in here. I'll need to search for it. I'll have to get some equipment though."

She nodded, and then spoke really quietly. "Where will you get that?"

"Dad. He'll courier to me today." He reached for his phone as it vibrated. "It's Dad. Let's see what he has to say." His face grew even grimmer. "This is not good, Leah. Someone is after you or after that treasure. Where's the information you have?"

"This way. I'll set you up here in the office. I have to do the cleaning and then prepare the afternoon tea. Come find me if you need me." She watched as he sank into her chair, his mind already on the papers in front of him, and sighed. Lord, you just had to send me someone like that, didn't You? I just know I'll fall in love with him and he'll walk away, taking my heart with him. She tried to seal her heart shut, but it was too late. Rory had already made inroads into it.

Rory stirred two hours later, looking at the notes he had made. He needed to see blueprints of the house before the renovation and now, as well as any blueprints or lot drawings. He stood, stretching, not sure where he was heading with what he found but knowing he just couldn't sit by and let her go through this on her own. It wasn't in him to walk away. He strode from the office, heading for the town, enjoying the warmth of the sun and the light breeze.

Leah stood on the wide wraparound porch, knowing Rory hadn't seen her and watched as he walked away. What had he found, Lord? What doesn't he want to tell me?

She sighed, before bending over the planters once more, her fingers working among the plants even as her thoughts drifted back over the last year or so, trying to pinpoint a time when she felt fear for the first time and not able to do that. It felt like she had been afraid for years and that was not how God wanted her to live.

She looked up later as she heard noise and frowned. No one should be in the house, all of her guests had dispersed to various activities. She shot a glance at the large antique Grandfather clock. Just coming up to noon, she thought. She hadn't heard Rory returning, so if that was the case, she thought, I'm here on my own.

She cautiously peeked into the various rooms, finally heading for the sunroom. Momentarily blinded by the light, she paused, not seeing the dark form heading her way until she felt a hand around her throat and was shoved up against the wall.

She heard the guttural words but couldn't understand them as she fought to free herself from the hand without success. She felt herself pulled away from the wall and then slammed against it, her head cracking back against it. She closed her eyes, slipping into the darkness creeping up on her, not hearing the questions hurled at her. She slumped to the floor finally as the man disappeared through the doors, leaving her in a crumpled heap.

Chapter 4

Whistling as he approached the Angel's Bed and Breakfast three hours later, Rory paused for a moment to study the rambling building and then lawns, gardens and outbuildings. It would be so easy for someone to destroy all this, he thought. He shook his head, knowing he wasn't planning on staying more than the month, not likely. He had found the town interesting to walk through, had listened to the gossip regarding Leah and her home, and then moved on to another store, to have it all repeated. He shuddered at some of the comments. Leah, what have you done? This is your home, but people don't like what you've gone and done to it. They resent the fact that you're moving on. I fear for you. Dear Lord, please, keep my new friend safe.

He stood for a moment on the porch, taking in the wicker furniture, the planters filled with brightly-colours flowers, the cushions in peach and jade. It was welcoming he thought. He frowned, hearing a cry from inside the house, and hit the solid wood door with the decorative etched window on a run, shoving it open and then sliding to a stop on the dark polished hardwood floor. Where had that scream come from?

He looked around, seeing Mrs. Townsend heading his way, her small statue literally shaking with fear.

"Mrs. Townsend?"

"Oh! You scared me! Come! Quick! Leah needs help!" She clutched for his arm, her arthritic fingers curling around his muscled forearm.

"What? Where is she?" He tampered down his urge to rush ahead, matching his steps to hers.

"In here. In the sunroom. She's not moving. I can't get her to wake up."

"Did you call for help?"

"Help? I did. You came!" She looked up at him, puzzled.

Rory sighed. "No, I meant did you call the police and an ambulance?"

"Oh! That help! Of course not. I haven't had time yet to do that. I found you instead."

"Mrs. Townsend? Here, you stay here and call the police. Dial 911. That will work. They will send someone." He set her down by the phone on the table in the living room, ensured that she was indeed doing what he asked, and then turned, heading rapidly for the sunroom.

He dropped to his knees beside Leah, a hand reaching out to brush back her hair. He grimaced as he saw the red marks on her neck as he reached a hand to check for a pulse. He sat back on his heels, his eyes roaming the room, seeking just what he wasn't sure. One thing he was sure of was that whoever had done this was long gone. That was a given.

He stood and stepped back as he heard heavy footsteps coming his way and a uniformed police officer stooped to check Leah before stepping back as more footsteps and the sound of wheels headed their way as well.

Rory watched and listened, knowing he couldn't step in. He had no right. He spoke with the officer and then pointed back at Mrs. Townsend, stating she was the one who had found Leah.

Leah stirred, her head pounding as she moved it. Confused, she blinked as she opened her eyes, staring at the booted feet around her and feeling hands on her head and neck. She shoved at them, pushing them away, and scrambled to her feet, fear taking over her actions. She spun, dizziness taking over, shaking off the hands that reached for her, seeing only one person who she felt safe with. She dodged the reaching hands and fled into Rory's arms, burrowing against him even as, shocked at her sudden appearance in front of him, he reached to encircle her with his arms and hold her close.

Pete Gallagher, the officer, shook his head. "No, that's not what we need, Leah. Please, have a seat on the gurney. The guys need to check you out."

She turned slightly, peering around Rory at him. "Absolutely not, Pete. I am not doing that." Her body swayed even as she spoke.

Rory shot a look at the officer, then scooped her into his arms and deposited her on the gurney, trying to step back but unable to release his shirt from her grasp. "Leah? It's okay. Just let them look you over. You need to do that. Please? For me?"

She finally subsided and let them assess her, adamant that she was not being taken to the hospital. She sat up abruptly, slipped from the gurney and found her way into Rory's arms again, turning so she was backed against him, her eyes huge, pain flickering across her face. "I can't. You need to leave now, please? It's time for me to put out the tea for my guests. If I need to, I see Doc Browne in the morning."

The first responders finally left, leaving Rory staring after them before he saw Mrs. Townsend standing there. He beckoned her forward, whispering in her ear. She gave a delighted nod and skipped away. He then turned to Leah, catching her arm as she turned on wobbly feet. He lead her into the kitchen and shoved her down in a chair, turning to reach for the jugs he knew she used for the juice.

Turning back, he sighed, shoving her back into her chair. "Would you stay put? Just tell me what you want put out. Mrs. Townsend was delighted to assist in the dining room today. Did you know she used to run a tearoom?"

"She did? Oh, how wonderful! Can I hire her to work her full time?" She turned as she heard quick footsteps.

Mrs. Townsend appeared, reaching into the fridge for the trays of sandwiches and fruit and vegetables. "I just might take you up on that, at least part time. I'm a widow, no children, no grandchildren. This town is just so perfect. I would love to stay here forever, my dear girl." She whirled away, heading for the dining room.

Leah stared after her before she turned back to Rory, her eyes narrowing as she caught him covering his mouth with his hand. "Just what did you say to her?"

"Just that we needed to keep what happened quiet and that you would need help." He studied her for a moment before walking to where she kept her coats and sorting through them, returning with a scarf, which he wrapped tenderly around her neck, ending up with a nice loop to it. "There, that hides the red marks."

"Red marks? Just what are you talking about?" She felt along the scarf, wincing as she hit the tender spots.

"Finger marks." He turned, a fine anger burning within him, before he looked back at her. He filled the kettles with hot water and coffee and headed for the dining room, where she could hear him gently teasing the older woman, his deep laugh warming her heart.

She watched as he came back and sat beside her, a hand reaching out to still the movement of hers. She waited, her eyes on his face, seeing the strength there but also a sadness. God, bless this man. Heal his heart.

Rory finally looked up, his eyes hurting as he nodded towards her neck. "Finger marks. He tried to kill you, Leah. I have no doubt about that. The officer that was here knows that too. He'll be back, trust me on that. He wasn't satisfied with having to leave like he did. He took pictures of your neck."

"He did? I didn't know that. Great! This is all I need. Word gets out and I'll have to shut down."

"Not necessarily. Become more involved in your community. That will help. Don't try to keep yourself apart. That's what I heard today. That you don't mingle, that you haven't for the last couple of years."

She nodded. "I know. It's been too hard." Her voice was barely above a whisper as she blinked back tears. "I lost my parents to a boating accident when I was about ten. Then two years ago, Grams went home. We don't know how. There was no evidence of any disease, heart issues. The coroner said it was like she had been scared to death or been drugged in some way. He was heartbroken he couldn't find the cause. Grams and Gramps were good friends of his own parents and they always treated him like one of theirs."

"That's interesting." Rory sat back, his hand still on hers, lost in thought. "I found some interesting items when I was researching. Can we talk tonight? I'll help out here in the dining room and kitchen.

Mrs. Townsend is in her glory out there. She'll just say you needed some help and asked her for it, given her history."

"That works.   But I can't let you help."   She went to rose and then sat back down, dizzy for a moment.

"Again, would you just stay put? Tell me what you want."

"Are you always this bossy?"   She shook her head, hiding a smile at his infectious grin. "I can see you are. How did your mother ever not let you away with anything?"   She blushed, realizing what she said, wishing to take back those words. Lord, put a lock on my tongue, please?

He just grinned at her.   "She has a secret weapon."

She tilted her head, a smile blooming on her face. "And that would be?"

"Dad."   He rose, heading for the dining room, hearing Mrs. Townsend speaking with the other guests.

"Your dad? Hey! Get back here! You can't say that and walk away." She watched him disappear through the swinging door. "But you just did.   Rory, what am I to do with you?" Her last words were whispered. She didn't want anyone to hear her.

Rory stood for a moment, letting the door swing back against him, his thoughts on the woman he had left in the kitchen. A spark was there, he noted, but given his history, he wasn't sure getting to know her better was a good idea. He watched as the other guests mingled, some sitting by themselves, others gathering in a group, Mrs. Townsend flitting among them. He grinned. This lady was something else, he thought. He knew she was in her late seventies, she had told him that as she flirted with him as they set up the tables. He had laughed at her nonsense, seeing some of his own grandmother in her words, knowing she was trying hard to cover her fright from earlier, and then had surprised her with a hug and a kiss to her cheek. She had stepped back, tears in her eyes, as she thanked him before she turned away.

Rory reached for a mug, filling it with coffee, and then reached for a plate to fill it with sandwiches. He looked behind him at the door to the kitchen, then filled a mug with tea, knowing that was what Leah liked. He headed back that way, finding her with her head on her folded arms, her shoulders shaking. He hesitated, not sure if he would intrude, then set the plate and mugs down, sliding into the chair he had vacated, and his arm going around her, his head bent near hers as he prayed for her.

Leah had stilled as she felt his arm around her, tensing for a moment, then relaxing as she heard his prayers, a peace filling her heart that she had not felt in years. She finally straightened up, feeling his hand move to cup her shoulder. She twisted slightly, her eyes on his, blinking to clear the tears.

"Thank you." She reached to drop a kiss on his cheek before she stood, moving to stand at the back door.

Rory sat where he was, his hands folded together on the table. He wanted to touch his cheek, but wouldn't. Not in front of her, not yet. Now, where did that thought come from? He shook his head. His father would tell him he was smitten, and he would have to agree. He rose, heading for the office, wanting to go over his research before they talked.

Mrs. Townsend appeared next to Leah, an arm around her. "How are you now, my dear?"

Leah shrugged, her hand on the scarf. "A little bit better. Thank you, Mrs. Townsend, for stepping in. I would like to talk to you tomorrow about hiring you, if you are sure."

"Tomorrow is fine. You need to get some sleep, my dear. But that young man of yours is waiting to talk to you, isn't he?"

"He is and he's not my young man."

"Not yet, but he will be. I can see that. Sleep well, my dear." She walked away, her footsteps light and quick.

Leah watched her go, then moved to pick up her trays to clear the tables in the dining room, finally turning from the full dishwasher she had started, and looked around. She sighed. Rory had brought them sandwiches, which neither of them had eaten. She reached for a tray, placing fresh mugs of coffee and tea and fresh plates of food on it, picking it up to head for the office, stopping as a thought ran through her mind. She set the tray back down and headed for the sunroom, looking around before she shook her head. No, it couldn't be, now could it?

She finally moved back to the kitchen, snagging the tray and heading for her office, setting it down on the low table near the couch and turning to find Rory standing beside her.

"Leah?"

"Yes, Rory? I'm puzzled about what happened today. Who was he?"

He motioned for her to sit and then handed her a plate of food. "Eat. We can talk afterwards. I'm starved for one." He bowed his head for a blessing on their food and then began to eat, finally pointing at her plate. "Eat something, please. I won't talk over anything with you until you do."

"Are you always this bossy?" She picked up a sandwich and began to nibble at it, taking a larger bite as her appetite kicked in.

He just grinned at her, his mouth full of food. When he swallowed, he hesitated before he spoke. "No, I don't think so. It's just that I've been in places where food was in short supply. You learned to eat when and where you could."

She watched him for a moment as she continued to eat. "Then, eat we will. But I still think you're bossy."

He laughed at that. "You do, do you?"

He finally wiped his hands on a napkin and sat back, his eyes on her. "Leah?" When she looked up, he saw the fatigue in her face. "How are you feeling?"

"Not the greatest. I have a really bad headache."

"Then, head off for bed. I'll clean up after us and lock up." He stood, a hand reaching out to pull her to her feet before he wrapped her into a hug and then sent her on her way, his eyes watchful. He turned back to his work, folding it away for the night before he walked through the house, securing the doors. It was late, he noted, frowning for a moment as he saw a flicker of light from the back garden. He reached for his jacket and headed that way. There should not be anyone out there, he knew.

Leah watched from her bedroom window as Rory headed for the back of the yard.   She had seen the same light and was concerned about his safety. She didn't know him well enough to know that he would and could protect himself. She realized she was thinking more and more about him in her life and that just wouldn't do. Not at all.

Chapter 5

Rory turned the next morning from the desk he had been sitting at, hearing Leah's footsteps heading his way. She had grudgingly agreed to meet him after she finished her work. He had politely told her that she needed to rest but she had refused, walking away from him to find her cleaning supplies

He watched as she adjusted the scarf around her neck. The same one from yesterday, he thought with a private grin. Now why wouldn't she have changed to another one?

She looked at him, then at the desk. "Now, we need to talk. What did you find?"

He looked down at his work, then back at her, before moving from the desk chair. "Here, you sit." He pushed her gently down, before he assessed her. "How's the head this morning?"

"It's there, if that's what you want to know.   It still hurts, but not as much as yesterday. Just what did you give me?"

He grinned.   "Just a simple herbal drink. It's something my Mom has used for years for headaches. She says it's a secret recipe but I'm sure she'd share with you."

"She would? She doesn't even know me."

"I know.   That's my Mom."   He reached for his phone as it vibrated, scanning the text message. "That was my Dad.   He's sending some information on your house to my email. I'll look at it later."

"You can look at it now, if you like." She shoved herself up from her chair, only to have him push her down gently once more. "Rory?"

"It's okay. He said it wasn't urgent, just some things I need to know, if I haven't already found them out."

"So what did you actually find out?" She was genuinely puzzled at his words, not sure what he had found, but knowing it would change her life in a drastic way.

"Okay. So, this house has been in your family for how long?"

She shrugged. "I don't know. At least from my great grandfather, I think. Grams would talk about being Gramps raised here." She searched his face. "Why?"

"How close are we to the lakes?"

"The Great Lakes? As in them?" At his nod, she blew out a breath. "Like, maybe five miles, give or take, depending on the tides and how much erosion there's been. Why?"

"Because I found stories about contraband and treasures that had been brought ashore from ships years ago." He smiled as she frowned at him. "Yeah, that." He shook his head as she continued to frown. "Didn't you know about that?"

"I guess. I just didn't expect it to be this far inland. I know the shore has receded over the years, so it would have been a longer haul, through forests and with no trail to get them here."

"Actually, there was a trail. It's your road now. It had just extended to the shoreline." He sorted through his papers, finding the map he was looking for and handing it to her. "Here. This is an old map, about one hundred and fifty years. I uploaded it to a photo program, made an overlay of it, and can show you how it's changed over the years."

"You can do that? Of course you can. Show me."

He reached for his laptop, pulling up the program and bringing up the modern map. "This is what your land looks like now. If I pull in the overlay this is what you would see." He watched as she traced the change with her finger. "It's quite a change, I would say."

"It is. How far would that have been then?"

"I can't say for sure, but more than your five miles of today. And don't forget, they didn't have the modern means of travel that we do. So this would have all been carried, whatever the treasure is."

"So you think someone is trying to scare me away from here, just so they can search?" She sat back, fear on her face. "Now I know what Grams meant. I thought she had been dreaming towards the end."

"What did she say?" He watched, concerned as her eyes slid closed and she thought back on her grandmother's words.

"She spoke of dark haired men searching outside. She even said she found them in the house one day and started locking up after that. I couldn't understand. I never said anything but I never saw them. I never found any evidence of them being around." She paused, a frown wrinkling her brow. "Or did I?"

"Did you what? See them? Find evidence?" His hand reached to lightly grasp her, still the movement of hers as she rubbed at the desk top.

"Evidence of them. I would find things moved around in the gardens. Signs that someone had been digging in the gardens. You know, that kind of stuff. I shrugged it off as animals or kids having fun." She stared at him, seeing the concern in his eyes. "I guess I shouldn't have?"

Rory shook his head. "Absolutely not. But then, you had no idea this was what they would be looking for." He shuffled through his papers, not finding the one he wanted at first.   "Here, this is what I've come up with."

She took it, her hand trembling somewhat as she searched his face before she looked down. Her face whitened. "Oh, my! All this? It can't be true. Surely over the years we would have found some of this."

Rory shrugged.   "Not necessarily. Unless you knew it was hidden somewhere here, you wouldn't think to look for it. I would hazard a guess that if there is something hidden, it's hidden well. There is not likely anything that would lead us to find it."

"That's scary, Rory.   How do I continue to operate my business under these circumstances?"   She rose and paced, her thoughts on her business and her guests. She turned as he didn't answer, watching him.

Rory finally looked up from his laptop, having read his father's email. "Dad has sent some documents for us to look at. I'll need to print them at some point. But first, what was on your agenda for today? What do we need to do around here?"

She shook her head. "You don't need to help, Rory. You're supposed to be working on setting up your new business, whatever that is."

"It can wait. You're more important than that." He watched as she flushed at his words, a thought running through his mind that he needed to be careful with her. Lord, lead my words. Don't let me hurt this beautiful lady.

She finally reached to touch his shoulder. "Okay then, let's go on with what you've found. That is if you want to."

He shrugged, clearly not wanting to answer. "You have work you need to do here. Don't you?"

She nodded. "I do have baking to do. Bring your research. We can talk while I work. That is, if you don't mind."

"As long as I get samples, I'm good with that." He just grinned as she shook a finger at him before she headed for the kitchen.

He was right behind her as she stopped abruptly, clutching his laptop and research tight to his chest to avoid dropping anything.

"Leah?" When she didn't respond, he spoke her name again, this time looking around her. "I'm guessing you didn't leave this mess?"

She shook her head. "Are you kidding me? Absolutely. I just love cleaning." Tears were near the surface as she took in the food thrown around the floor, all her hard work of cooking and baking destroyed. "Now, what am I do to? It's almost time for tea and I have nothing ready." She sank to the floor, her hands covering her face.

Rory stepped around her to set his work down, and then he stared around, finally reaching for a garbage pail, broom and dustpan. He just quietly starting cleaning up the mess.

She rose, her hand on her face as she stared at the mess, at him and then at the fridge. Determination took over and she ran for the freezer. "Yes!" She began to pull bags of cookies ready to bake from depths of her freezer, rolls that she had baked. She searched and found meat she could use. Whoever had tried to run her tea had just lost, she thought. Thank you, Lord, that You prompted me to do this.

Rory turned from washing his hands, his head going into the fridge and then he turned to her, a nod at what she had accomplished coming her way. "That's the spirit. There is some fresh fruit in here. We could do a salad with that. Here's cucumbers, tomatoes." He searched further. "And onions. I know a salad I can make from these, if you have oil and vinegar for me."

"In that cupboard, there in the pantry." She was racing against time she knew but she was determined to have her tea out on time.

An hour later, she stood, watching as her guests exclaimed at the daintiness of Rory's salad, at the fresh hot rolls and butter, the selections of meat she had provided, the fruit Rory had worked over.

Mrs. Townsend approached her. "This is just so wonderful, my dear. Such a variety of foods you have provided for us. Something so simple as this? It's a refreshing change of pace for us all."

Leah watched, mouth open, as she moved away. Rory tapped under her chin, causing her mouth to close, a grin on his face.

"We make a good team, you know. Now, if we could only solve the problems you're facing, you'd be all set."

She followed the movements of the guests for a moment, listening to their conversation and the laughter, and then shook her head at him. "You have a way with words, do you know that? I was ready to give up until you took over in there. Your encouragement got me moving."

Rory stared at her for a moment, and then clasping her arm, drew her back into the kitchen. "What I want to know is who did this and why didn't we hear them?"

"I know. When I came to find you, the kitchen was spotless and I had everything ready for tea." She sighed, looking at the clock. "I have to bake tonight yet."

Rory's hand stopped her movement. "Plan something simple for the morning, and I'll be up to help you bake." He grinned at her frown. "What? You don't think I can? Now, is the grocery store still open?"

"It is. Why? You making a food run, afraid you won't get anything to eat?"

He laughed. "No, we are. We're heading there to replace your fruit and vegetables. Then you have an early night. You need it. I suspect you haven't been sleeping well, now have you?"

Unable to admit he was right, and that she was terrified, she turned away, heading for her bedroom to collect her purse. When she returned, he was just putting away the mop, having washed the floor for her.

"I told Mrs. Townsend that she could leave the dishes, but she's determined to earn her keep."

"Thank you, Rory. You would think you had been here for ever."

He flushed, grateful for her words. "No, I'm just used to problem solving."

"And that problem solving will solve my problems?" She smirked as he hit the brakes, an astonished look on his face before he began to laugh.

"My, my. It didn't take long for the sarcasm to come back." He grinned at her again, glad to help, but wanting so much more, he decided.   Lord, I have no idea where this is going, but this lady needs Your protection.   Help me to solve this for her. He watched closely as she maneuvered her way through the store, a quick smile and word for those she met.

He paused as he was closing the trunk lid of his car, his hand resting for a moment on the metal, as he watched her through the back window. She doesn't see it, does she, Lord?   How well liked she is in this town? It's not the townspeople who are causing her issues, not the ones anyway that I've met in Angel's Bay.   There are some who resent her. So who is it? Guide us as we search and provide protection for her. He shivered as thoughts muddled in his mind, his eyes raised to search around him, a habit he had picked up that he just couldn't or wouldn't put down.

Chapter 6

Two days later, Rory stood on a large rock, part of a huge rock formation at what the locals called Angel's Bay. He stared around, not quite sure what he was looking for, but entranced with the rugged beauty of the area. He squinted, his mind trying to fathom what it would have been like there two hundred years ago. He turned as he heard his name called. Leah stood there, her eyes on him, a hand shadowing her face.

"Be careful, Rory. Don't fall, please."

He jumped down and approached her, a grin on his face. "What makes you think I'd fall?"

"It's been known to happen here. Spooky things. Some say this place is haunted, that the ghost of a previous mariner killed by his crew still wanders here." She shuddered at the thought.

He reached to tug her towards him, wrapping her in a hug, that ended too soon

64

as far as he was concerned, Leah moving away from him, her eyes on the water.

"Rory? What's that?"

"What's what?" He paused beside her, not seeing what she was pointing at.

"That. It looks like a metal box. I don't remember seeing anything like that here before."

He walked towards the water, his hand keeping her back. "Just wait a minute, Leah. Don't go rushing in. We have no idea what that is."

"No, we don't, and we won't until we open it." She studied it and then him. "Well? What are you waiting for? Christmas?"

He shot her a glance and then began to laugh. "Christmas? That's what seven or eight months away? I can wait that long. I just don't think you can."

She stared at him for a moment, finally seeing the mischief sparkling in his eyes and the grin he was trying hard to hide but which he was unsuccessful in doing. "Yes. Christmas. Don't they say that where you from?"

"No, I don't think they do. It's more like the phrase, hold your horses." He laughed openly as she continued to stare at her.

Removing his shoes and socks and rolling up his jean legs, Rory stepped cautiously into the clear water. "It's cold!"

She began to laugh. "It is. The lake always is. Well? Can you reach it or are you too much of a wimp?"

"A wimp." He raised his hands, staring at the sky. "Hear that? She just called me a wimp!" He listened to her musical laughter, knowing he could listen to it forever. He reached for the box, tugging it free from the crevice it had become wedged in. He waded back towards her, his eyes raising to meet hers and then tracing behind her. He gave a sudden yell and launched himself at her, taking her to the ground again, and using his body to cover hers.

She struggled against him, only laying still when he hissed a warning at her. He raised his head, searching for the assailant and not seeing him. He rolled to the side, his hand going out to help her sit up.

"Rory? Just what was that all about?" She felt anger burning within her, even though she knew it was wrong.

"That!" He reached for the metal box, pointing to the hole drilled into it. "He was shooting at you."

She paled, her eyes growing huge as she stared at the box. "That?" She began to shake, fear taking over for a moment. "That's from a bullet? Rory? Who?"

"I have no idea." He sprang to his feet, pulling her up and reaching for the box. "Let's head back to your place. I don't want you out in the open any more than I can prevent that." His hand clasped hers tight, leading her away from the bay and towards her home. He paused as he neared the trees, his eyes scanning the ground, seeing nothing overt, but then he really didn't expect to.

"Rory?" She waited beside him, watching him closely. "Who would do this?"

He shrugged. "That I don't know. What I do know is that they've upped the ante in the game and you are now a target. You must know something and not realize that you do." He walked forward, drawing her with him, the box under his arm. "We'll open this once we get back to the B&B."

She sighed. "I know we will. But do we want to?"

"What do you mean?" He glanced quickly at her, seeing a distant look in her face.

"I've seen that box before. It was my Grandfather's. He left it in the attic. I haven't been up there in a couple of months so I didn't know it was missing."

"That changes everything. We'll need to speak with the police again."

She violently shook her head. "No, not that. I can't."

"And just why not?" Rory felt the frustration mounting in him as he swung the door to the house open for her.

"Because they think I'm making everything up."

"They can't deny a bullet. That will still be inside."

"Oh, but they can. They'll say I did it." She shivered despite the warmth of the day.

"And do you own a gun? Have you ever fired one?"

She shook her head. "I'm so afraid of them. Grams wouldn't have one in the house." She watched as he reached for a piece of newspaper to set the box on. "Just what do you think is in it?"

He shrugged as he bent over it, leaning around to study it. "It hasn't been in the water long. Likely just overnight." He paused, his eyes on her. "What did your grandfather keep in it?"

"I have no idea. I just know it was his. I haven't gone through anything in the attic yet. I haven't had the heart to do that."

She watched as he worked to open it. "Someone has tried hard to get it open. Do you know if there's a key around for it?"

She paused, lost in thought, before reaching into a drawer near the sink. "It should be on this ring. It was his. Grams just kept it here, for memory's sake, and I haven't had the heart to move it."

With a quiet thank you, he worked the key into the battered lock and finally felt a click. He stood hands on the box, his heart lifted in prayer, knowing that when he opened it, it would likely change her life in a way she wasn't prepared for or expecting.

"Rory?" Her quiet voice reached him and he looked up.

"You're sure you want to open this?"

Leah nodded. "I need to. Whatever it contains, I need to know. Someone went to a lot of work to take it."

His hand reached for hers, stilling her motions. "When this is done, I want your tools. I need to put a lock on that attic door for you. It will not likely keep anyone out but it would slow them down and maybe make them think twice about going in there, especially if they had to break down the door. It would be way too noisy."

"It would at that." She drew in a deep breath and pushing his hand off the box, pulled the metal container to her. A sadness wafted through her. *Gramps, I have no idea what you had in here. It may be nothing. It may be something.* She opened it slowly, her hand freezing as she held the lid.

"Leah?" Rory moved to stand beside her, his eyes on her face. "Leah?"

She shook herself and looked at him. "It's a diary. I remember him writing in one every once in a while. But what would it contain that someone would want?"

She reached to pull the small black leather-bound book from the box, turning it over and over in her hands. "No, this isn't his. It's too old."

Rory leaned against the table, a finger touching the leather. "It is. I would say at least one hundred years or more, given the binding on it."

"And how do you know that?"

He gave a tight smile. "My mother deals in antiquities, particularly old books. I spent a lot of time with her when I was a teen, thinking I wanted to do what she did." He sighed. "Life happens and plans change."

She shoved the book at him. "Here. You open it. I can't." She looked down into the box. "And here we have the bullet. Rory, what do we do with it?"

"Seal the box and the bullet into a box, date it and then lock it into your safe. You do have a safe, don't you?"

She shook her head. "Actually, no, I don't." She suddenly slapped herself on her forehead, astonishing Rory. "I do. I keep forgetting that I do."

Rory began to laugh. "Well, which is it? Do you or don't you?"

She swatted at him, a grin hovering on her face. "I do. I just have never used it. Here, seal your box in this. There's a marker. Then follow me."

He watched as she reached to the floor, pulling aside a small mat and then dialed a combination. "This is interesting."

"It is. Gramps said his father put it in, back when they kept their money and jewelry at home rather than in a bank." She reached for the box, tucking it away and then pausing. "Here, let me lift out these ledgers. We may find something in them."

Rory took then, turning to set them on her desk, before turning back, dropping to his knees beside her. "What else is in there?"

"Nothing that I can see. Just those ledgers." She sat back on her heels. "But I feel like I am missing something, something important."

He reached a hand to help her stand, walking over to touch the ledgers with a long lean finger. "What are these?"

"I forget. Gramps told me about them at one time." She spun as she heard a sound, her hand going to her throat before she caught sight of the clock. "Oh, no. Not again. Rory, lock those in my desk, please? I have to put tea out."

"Right behind you." He watched as she scampered from the room, as he thought of her movements, before shaking his head and then reaching to lock the ledgers away before he stood, his eyes on the desk and then raised to the windows. Something was off and he wanted to find out just what before he went after her.

Rory felt along the window frame, pausing as his fingers hit a raised portion, before nodding. He shot a look behind him as he pulled out his pocket knife. Either another camera or a listening device, of that he was sure. Now, this was not good. He dug out the object before he pocketed his knife and what he had dug out and then returned to the desk, unlocking it and pulling the ledgers from it. He headed for his own room, tucking the books away in what he hoped was a safe place and then paused, his eyes on his briefcase. He sighed. He would need to look at that phone today, he knew that. But later, he thought. Right now, a beautiful young lady who had enchanted his heart needed his help.

Leah looked around for Rory later that night. He had casually mentioned that he had moved the ledgers, thinking it for the best. She had stared at him for a moment, seeing the concern and caring in his eyes and just nodded. Now, she needed to find him and see what his thoughts were.

Rory looked up from the swing he begun to think of as his. He reached for her hand, pulling her down beside him, her hand tight in his as he shoved a toe against the floor to move the swing. He liked this time of day, twilight, with the twittering of the birds settling for the night, the night insects taking over for the day insects, the sound of the frogs from the pond near the back of the property. It's peaceful, he thought, knowing that he suddenly wanted to stay there, to have Leah near him for the rest of their lives, to find what he was looking for after all.

She rested for a moment, her eyes on his face, before they dropped to their linked hands. "Rory? Where are the ledgers?"

"I tucked them away somewhere. I don't want to say out loud where. I'm not sure how many more cameras or listening devices there are. I found one on the office window after you left."

She paled at his words. "You did?" Her voice was low and almost panicked. "What have I done?"

"You, my dear, have done nothing. Except try to make a new life and living for yourself. Somehow, someone found out about the supposed treasure and is determined to destroy what you've created for yourself to find it."

"That is true. I just don't get it. We never had any riches. Just what we've earned. Gramps always said his father was approached at one time to take in contraband and he refused." She turned her head to study the horizon, watching as the stars began to twinkle brightly in the dark blue of the night sky. She too listened to the music of the night, it calming her in a way little could. "Dad always said he thought there was a treasure here, but then, he'd quote the Bible, that where your treasure was, that's where your heart was. He always made sure I knew what treasure to seek. Mom always told him he treated us like his treasure. He would just laugh and hug her and then me, saying we were his treasure."

"That's so sweet, Leah. Dad doesn't put it quite like that, but I know that's what he means when he says we have to make a decision about what is the most important thing in life for us."

"It sounds like our fathers shared a faith. I'm glad." She leaned back again, her eyes on his face. "What are you thinking, Rory?"

Rory shrugged. "I'm not quite sure. I need to do some more research. We still have to go over what I've already found. And then there's that journal or diary."

"And the ledgers." She hesitated, not quite sure how to frame her thoughts.

"And you're afraid that those journals will show something you are not prepared to see, aren't you?"

She nodded. "I am. I guess I don't want anyone to look down on my family."

"Family is important but it is the past. I know someone will look down on you no matter what we find."

"That's too true."

The following morning, Rory stood for a moment, watching as Leah tidied the dining room, reaching to take the used linens from her. He headed for her laundry room, despite her protest, and started the washer, turning when it was set to find her standing in the doorway, a dark look on her face.

"That's not necessary, Rory. You have stuff of your own to do."

He simply grinned. "Nothing is as important at you are at this moment. Now, can you spare some time?"

"I can. Is it all right if we work in the kitchen? I have some baking to do, but I can multitask."

"That we can do. Let me get my notes and the books." He waited until she shifted from the doorway, watching as she walked towards the kitchen, noticing the slumping of her shoulders that signified discouragement.   Lord, she needs You. Protect her.

Leah stood for a moment, her eyes on the doorway behind her, hearing Rory's footsteps fade away before she sighed.   She was beginning to depend on him too much, she thought, and then shook her head.   It's not like he was giving her an option.

Chapter 7

Setting down the books, Rory headed for the coffee pot, then paused. He was beginning to feel very much at home here, with Leah, and that puzzled him, causing him to shake his head before he moved back to the counter with his mug of coffee. He set it down before sliding onto one of the stools there, his hands reaching for the books. He glanced through them, setting them into order. He was surprised at the details he saw.

Leah watched for a moment, before she busied herself with her baking. It had to be done, regardless. That was a given, she thought. Lord, she prayed, I have no idea what is upcoming or even what those books hold. You do. Let me rest in You today, letting my burdens and worries go to you and not overwhelm me.

"What did your grandfather do for a living?" Rory's voice broke into her thoughts.

"He was a blacksmith. The barn out back still has his tools and the forge. Why?" She looked up at him, a question on her face.

"I'm just trying to get a sense of your family, as to why someone would want to harm you. What about his father?"

"He farmed, fished. Just about anything I think he needed to do to provide for his family. It was a different life back then. Not many, other than merchants, worked off their own property." She paused. "Dad always said he would have liked to experience life back then. He worked with Gramps in the shop until he died in that accident."

"What accident?" Rory looked up sharply, a narrowed look on his face.

"He was in a boating accident. He and Mom. Out in Angel's Bay. For some reason their boat took on water and sank, taking them with it. I could never figure out why they were out there that late at night."

Rory drew in a deep breath. "Are you sure it was an accident?"

She nodded. "The police investigated and said that's what it was. Why? You don't think so?"

"It's just something we need to look at. I'll have Dad pull the report for us through the business. It will work better that way than my asking for it. You don't happen to have a copy?"

She thought for a moment as she turned to wash her hands and dry them, hanging the towel back up on the hook. "Grams or Gramps might have. I'll go take a look. I know they were keeping a file they wouldn't show me. I haven't had to heart to go through." She was gone and back in short order with a thick file folder in her hands. "There's more here than I thought."

"Thank you, my dear. Now, can you sit for a moment?" He watched as she glanced at the clock before she nodded, sliding onto the stool next to him. He gave a low growl and was up on his feet, making her the herbal tea he knew she favoured, setting her favourite cup in front of her before he sat back down and reached for the folder she had set in front of him.

Leah's look of surprise and then pleasure was missed by him. She had not been treated like that in years, not by a man. Her Gramps used to do that for her and Grams, dropping a kiss on their temple as he did so. She swallowed against the sudden lump in her throat before she spoke.

"What are you looking for, Rory?"

"The police report for one. Do you have a marine patrol here?"

"In the next town. I'm sure they were called in. I was young, about ten, when it happened."

"That's too young to lose your parents." He searched through the paperwork, finally seeing the report. He perused it. "There's not much here. Other than the date, the time the report of them being missing came in, details of who was in on the search." He read further. "It just says that the boat sank in still waters for an unknown reason." He reached for photos, staring at them. "Do you have a magnifying glass?" He reached for the one she hunted up for him, setting it against one photo. "There. That's what they didn't say."

"What? Rory, what didn't they say?"

He didn't answer for a moment, searching for the marine patrol report. "Here we go. More details. That's strange. Their report states a hole in the side of the boat, just at the water line. That's not in the police report and it should be."

"What does that mean? Someone sabotaged it?"

He nodded, looking up with a look of compassion as she drew in a deep breath. "It seems so. Let me see if the coroner's report is there." He leafed through the pages. "This is strange. There are no reports and they should be here."

"They're not? I remember Grams talking about getting them." She sat back, a frown on her face, a frown that Rory suddenly wanted to kiss away and make her smile again.

He swallowed hard, looking back at the folder, his fingers sorting the papers even as his mind tried to sort through his feelings. "If you don't have it, Dad can pull it to. I think we need to send this on to him, let him start an official investigation. You have grounds to do just that."

"Your father? He would do that without even meeting me? Just what does he do anyway?"

He looked up, knowing he would have to confess what he was running from, and not sure he wanted to but he needed to. "My father runs an investigation firm, usually moving in to retrieve people from situations they find themselves in. That can happen here in this country, in a neighbouring country or more often in a hostile country."

"You did that, didn't you? What happened that chased you away from that? You loved that thrill of adventure, didn't you?" She watched the bleak look come over his face and noted that he didn't shutter his feelings this time.

"I did love it, Leah, but when the last job went south, as they say, and the person I was to bring back was killed before I reached them, I had to walk away to get some perspective back. I'm not sure I can even go back to that line of work." He gave her a cheeky grin. "I'm sort of beginning to like the B&B business."

She stared at him, her mouth open before she snapped it closed. "You do, do you? And just why?"

He shrugged, not able to put into words his feelings. "I have no idea. Maybe it's the B&B owner that makes a difference." He didn't look at her, just keep a small grin on his face as he heard her sputtering before he stared down at the paper he has just unearthed, the grin fading quickly.

"Rory?" When he didn't answer, she leaned against his arm, reading the paper he had found. "What is that? A threat?"

"It appears to be. Directed at first your father, then his name stroked out and your grandfather's put in place. What is this treasure they are asking about and demanding they turn over?"

"I have no idea. We have no treasure. Never have had. My family have worked hard for everything they have. They always have done that." She reached for some of the paperwork, flipping it through it, a frown still on her face. "I don't get this. What are they after?"

Rory reached for the first ledge. "Let's take a look at this. Maybe it will help us."

An hour later, having worked their way through the ledgers, and finding nothing to help explain, Rory sat back, his eyes on Leah as she moved around her kitchen, setting away her baking, preparing what she needed to do, and knowing he felt content and at peace for the first time in years.

He reached for his phone as it vibrated. It was his father. "Dad? Hi. No, I'm fine. You guys? That's good. He said what? Tell him I'm not coming home. I like it here." He rose, moving to find a pen and paper. "What can you tell me? I see. No, that does makes sense, in a twisted way. We have been going over paperwork. You offered to set up an investigation. It's time we did. I'll forward copies of everything on to you, but I have found irregularities all ready. The police report. There is no coroner's report. The marine patrol report is different from the official police report." He glanced at Leah, to see her standing against the counter, arms folded across her abdomen, as she watched him and listened to his side of the conversation. "Leah? She's good with this. At least, that's what she said. I know. Okay. I'll get these to you as soon as I can." He paused as he listened for a moment, his eyes dropping to the ledgers. "Dad, we have ledgers that I'm not sure what to think about. No, just daily or weekly listings of business or farm animals or whatever they were involved with. Nothing that would mean anything other than to the family. I just don't see why they've been kept."

He finally pocketed his phone, reaching to gather the material, before he spread it out again, his phone out once more as he began to take pictures of everything.

"Rory? What did your father say?" Leah moved to stand beside him, her hand reaching out to still his.

"He said, given what I told him and what we're finding, and then that shot at you yesterday, we need to open an investigation. In fact, he has already done just that."

"He has? Without asking? How can he?" She tamped down the brief feeling of anger, knowing it was unwarranted.

"Because I'm here. Because he says he can hear I care about you. Anyone we care about automatically become family and family is always put first. That's how Dad is. So, once he heard about the shooting, he just went ahead. He would not have done much though, if you had not agreed."

She finally walked away, to spin and come back at him. "And you would have told me? You wouldn't have just gone ahead and investigated?"

He rose, to walk towards her, finally drawing her into a tight hug, feeling the shudders running through her. "No, I would not have done that. Dad would have only go so far, and wouldn't have investigated anything if I had asked him not to." He just held her, feeling her tears soaking his shirt, as he rocked her gently in his arms. "Dad said he's heading this way tomorrow. He wants to see what we have."

She nodded, then sighed. "But I have no room. They are all booked up."

He grinned at her concern, knowing she couldn't see him. "That's okay. He'll bunk with me if he has to stay overnight. It wouldn't be the first time."

She finally moved away and Rory stood, feeling like he had just lost her. "Leah? Are you sure you're okay with this?"

She nodded, not looking at him, so he didn't see the tears on her cheeks, tears she vowed not to show him. "I am. Just keep me in the loop as they say." She walked away, heading for the dining room.

He listened for the songs she usually sang as she worked, but there was no music, no humming, no singing. He sighed. Lord, what did I do that I shouldn't have done? He reached to gather the material up, staring once more at the police report, a frown covering his face. Who wrote this and what were they trying to cover up? He feared suddenly for Leah, knowing that once word got out they were investigating her parents' death and how it related to what she was going through, she would be in even more danger. That he would try to avoid but knew it would be impossible.

Chapter 8

Staring at the tall older gentleman standing in front of her registration desk the next morning, Leah drew in a deep breath, her eyes shooting towards the kitchen. Rory was in there, so it wasn't him standing in front of her. The man was so like him, it had to be his father.

"Hi! You must be Leah? Rory described you very well." The man grinned at her, and she suddenly relaxed.

"That would be me. You must be Rory's father."

"And that would be me." He grinned at her again as he copied her words, drawing an answering smile from her. "Hi. I'm Riordan Stuart. You can call me Dad if you like." He laughed as her mouth dropped open, just as the door opened behind her.

"Dad? What mischief are you up to now?" Rory stood beside Leah, his head tilted to watch her face flush.

"Me? I'm never up to mischief, Rory. You should know better." He reached around the counter to hug his son and then stood, an arm around his shoulders as he looked around. "This is nice. Homey, comfortable, yet professional. Whoever your designer was, they deserve to have their work showcased in a magazine." He looked at Rory as he choked on his laughter. "Now, what did I say?"

"Leah's the designer, Dad. She did most of the work herself as well." Rory watched as Leah flushed at his praise.

"She did? Well, then I want to hire you to redo our offices. They need updating. You'll be perfect." He moved away as Leah sputtered at his words, catching Rory's look of sympathy and quickly suppressed grin.

"Did he just say that?" Her words were hissed at him.

"He did and he meant every word. Now, what do we have to do for this afternoon's tea?"

She had given up trying to get him not to help. It just wasn't working. He would go ahead even though she told him not to.

"I have the tablecloths and napkins to put out and then the flowers to arrange. You could do that." She smirked as he shook his head. "No? Not the flowers? I'm surprised. I thought you would want to do those." She headed for the kitchen, Rory heading the other way to find his father.

"Dad?" When Riordan turned to face him, Rory drew in a deep breath. "You've found something."

"I have, son, and I do need to talk to you both. Rory. Just one question. Where is your heart in all this?" Riordan watched with compassion as his son struggled to find words. "That's what your Mom and I thought. Our prayers are for your protection and guidance. Just let us know how we can help. Now, if you'll send me the way of our shared abode, I'll get out of your hair and sort through what I've brought with me."

Three hours later, Riordan watched as both Rory and Leah interacted with the guests, seeing how well Rory had fit in. He sighed, knowing he had lost his son to the business, but happy for him. He prayed Rory would know where he wanted to be and then follow through. Leah, he thought, you are good for him. You challenge him, but support him in an understated way that builds him up at the same time. That's what Naomi does for me, he realized.

Rory finally approached his father, his manner thoughtful but hesitant. "Dad? We just have to clean up and then we can talk."

"You two haven't eaten, and I just had tea.   Does she have a grill and some chicken? I can do our meal for us."

"I do, Mr. Stuart." Leah spoke from beside him. "This way."

His hand on her arm stopped her movement and she studied his face even as he was shaking his head. "Please, call me Riordan. Mr. Stuart was my father."

She laughed at him and nodded. "I guess I can do that. If you'll follow me, I'll show you where everything is."

She watched as Riordan headed for her patio, tray of meat in hand, before she turned, finding Rory watching her, a look on his face she couldn't read, but one that made her feel treasured and special.

"He's just taking over, isn't he?" Rory grinned. "He does that. He'll stay for a few days, looking into things. And don't worry. No one will figure out what he's up to." He moved towards her, his hands coming up to cup her shoulders. "I know that this is all upsetting and nerve-wracking and frightening. Let Dad work his magic and see what he discovers."

"It's not like I have much choice." She sounded disgruntled even to her own ears and she sighed. "I'm sorry. That's not nice. That is also not what I wanted to say."

"No, it's okay. Dad does kind of take over. If you ask, he'll step back. But he thinks best when his hands are busy. So we'll let him think it over. Have you any more thoughts?"

She went to shaker her head, and then stopped. "The attic. I've never looked much through it, just moved things around as I needed to. Maybe we need to search up there."

"We can do that. Do you have thirty minutes right now? It would be a start."

She glanced at the clock. "As long as it's not much more than that, then yes." She was surprised when he grabbed her hand and pulled her to the stairs. "Wait, I need the key." She ran back for it, coming towards him, finding his hand outreached to take hers again.

Rory stood in the attic, staring at the mess. "I don't think this is how you left this."

"No, absolutely not." Leah turned slowly in a circle. "It was nice and tidy when I had the locksmith up here. I was up here after to check the door and it was fine."

"Then someone has picked the lock." He bent to look at it. "I can see fine scratches on it, so that's what they have done."

Sighing, Leah looked around. "I have to put everything back, and it will take longer than the thirty minutes I promised you."

"Let's get started and see how far we can get. The boxes are still intact, so that is a bonus."

"It is. Do you always look on the bright side of life?"

He just grinned. "Not all the time. Today, for you, my dear, I do."

She reached for his wrist, turning it so she could see the watch. "Oh, dear. I need to get downstairs. And I'm sure your father had our meal ready."

"He'd come find us if he did. Head on down. I'll work up here for a bit longer, and then be down." Rory watched her walk away, his heart hurting for her but fearing for her as well. Lord, I have no idea what she's facing coming up, but You do and You are there. Please, dear Lord, surround her.

Riordan appeared in the doorway, having been sent that way by Leah. "Wow! She said it was a mess. But you two have been cleaning right?"

"We have been, Dad." Rory sat back on the floor, leaning on his hands, his legs stretched out in front of him as he contemplated what they hadn't got to. "She really doesn't know what is up here, though, other than it was family stuff." He looked around, then up to his father. "You came up for a reason other than to tell me it's a mess?"

Riordan grinned, looking very much like his son at the moment. "Well, I could tell you it's a mess, but we already did." He stooped to pick up a picture, a frown on his face. "Now, this man looks familiar."

"That's my father. Why? Did you ever meet him?" Leah stood in the doorway, a hand to her throat, hope in her face.

"I think I did. Years ago at a conference. He looks so familiar." He paused, his eyes on his son. "I'll have to go back through some photos, but I think I have one on him from then. It would be about twenty years ago."

"That would be just before he died." Leah spun and ran down the stairs, her feet barely touching the steps.

Rory was on his feet, heading for the door as his father spoke. "This is what will continue to happen, Rory. Just so you know, son. Be prepared to comfort her and challenge her to continue to seek for answers. If you don't, she'll pack away everything and not move forward. And she needs to do just that."

Rory paused, turning to face his father. "I know, Dad. That's what I want to do, encourage her and keep her moving forward. If she doesn't, this place will close and she'll have nothing to fall back on."

Riordan watched as his son rapidly descended the stairs, before he sighed, stepping through the door before he closed it and locked it, his eyes on the key in his hand. "There has to be a key in here somewhere, Lord, that will unlock all this. Please, dear Lord, lead us to it? And with no harm to my son or his lady."

Riordan followed the younger couple down the stairs, stopping for a moment in the dining room doorway to watch Leah move among her guests, listening to her laughter and her teasing them, but he could hear the fear and stress underlying it. Rory watched her as well, his heart on his face. Riordan sighed. I know I need to talk to him too, dear Lord, but what can I say he hasn't already said to himself.

Rory approached his father, plates in hand for their supper from the grill, and sighed. "You have that look on your face, Dad."

"Which one is that?"

"The one that says you need to talk to me but don't know how to."

Riordan paused for a moment, tongs in hand, before he reached for the grilled chicken, cobs of corn and potatoes he had prepared. "I do, don't I? I want to talk to you, son, about something, but it's personal and private between us. Later?"

Rory nodded as he sensed Leah approaching him, ready to take the plates from him and set them on the patio table. He watched for a moment, not aware that his father's eyes were first on him and then on the young woman.

"Riordan, thank you. This means a lot. I haven't had someone prepare a meal like this since Grams went home." Leah sat, watching as the men sat and then each reached for her hands before Riordan asked the blessing on their food.

"Leah? What happened in the attic?" Riordan paused for a moment mid-meal, his eyes on her.

She shrugged. "I have no idea. It wasn't like that four days ago, wasn't it, Rory, when the locksmith changed the lock. Rory said it looks as if someone picked the lock."

"That's my impression. And that's difficult to do. You don't leave here much.

I know you spend time in the yard, don't you?"

"Some, but I've had to hire a landscaper to look after the outdoors this year. I've been too busy inside and getting the business running." She paused, her eyes on her plate, not seeing the looks the two men exchanged. "I couldn't do justice to the beds. John's been a friend for years and has his own business. Maybe talk to him and ask if he saw anyone."

"We can do that." Rory shoved back his plate, his appetite gone. "Now, those ledgers."

"Yes, the ledgers. They don't contain anything other than normal daily life from years ago. From an historical point of view, they are valuable." Rory looked at his father. "Did you find anything unusual, Dad?"

Riordan brought his thoughts back to the present. "There was something there. I asked Sam to look into it. He'll report to me when he finds something. Someone is after an object, journal, whatever it is they think you have. Until we find it or them, you are in danger, Leah. Make no doubt about that."

He nodded at Rory. "Rory's being here is something I'm glad off. God prepared that. He wasn't supposed to be coming this way."

Rory began to laugh. "No, I wasn't. I was heading the opposite way until Mom happened upon your advertisement. She persuaded me I had to come this way, that Angel's Bay B&B was just too good to be missed. I must say. She was right. Once more. Don't tell her that, Dad."

Riordan broke out into laughter, bringing laughter from his son and a questioning look from Leah. "It's okay, Leah. Naomi does these things, finds places or people, persuades us we need to have them in our lives. She's usually right on." He rose and began to clear their plates away, much to Leah's distress.

Rory's hand on her arm kept her still. "Just let him, okay? It's what he does and it distresses him if people protest too much." He rose as well, heading for the kitchen and returning with the tray of squares and cookies and their tea that she had left prepared.

She watched, not used to be waited on, uncomfortable at first until Rory's hand settled on her shoulder and she relaxed, not seeing the speculative look sent their way by Riordan.

"What's next in the investigation?" Leah finally broke into the silence.

"I want to go back over the ledgers, look through the journal of your grandfather, and then take a look in the attic. There must be something there." He frowned. "I also want to go over the whole house."

"And for what reason? I have my guests' privacy to think of."

Riordan nodded. "I realize that. I doubt you would find anything in the guest rooms. It will be in your quarters, the common areas, the hallways. I'll look around tomorrow when they've gone out for the day." He paused again. "Is there one guest who seems insistent on helping you, being around you?"

Rory and Leah exchanged a glance before Leah sighed, frustration evident. "Amy Townsend. I've been using her help in the dining room. I guess I shouldn't have."

"Just let me have what information you have on her and we'll look into it."

"I'll get it for you in the morning." She yawned. "I'm sorry. My day starts early and it's already been a long day." She rose, heading for the kitchen with the tray, leaving the men staring after her.

Chapter 9

Looking for his father the next day, Rory searched the B&B, even heading up to the attic. He paused in the doorway before looking back down the stairs. He finally walked forward, his hands reaching for clothing to fold and replace in trunks, feeling around in the trunks for any hidden sections and finding now.

He then stood, his eyes tracking along the walls, not seeing anything overt but knowing something could well be there. He ran his hands along the low walls and paused at one section. The wall felt different. He felt along the edge and heard a small click. He pulled at it, and looked inside, feeling around, pulling out old rolled maps and two small metal boxes. He set them aside and felt once more around the crevice before he carefully closed the opening and then sat on the floor, his eyes on what he had found, before he stood, gathering the material and heading to find

Leah. These needed to be locked away in her safe, that he had no doubt about.

She looked askance at what he was holding before nodding and drying her hands on a towel. She opened the safe, not questioning what he had. He had shaken his head at her, not wanting to say much. He kept the conversation on other topics and she complied with unspoken request on his face.

When they had returned to the kitchen, he poured himself a cup of coffee and sat at the breakfast bar, his phone out as he looked over his messages, seeking for something that would solve this and finding none. He felt her hand on his shoulder and looked up, seeing something on her face that gave him a tiny ray of hope that she might care for him.

"Rory? What is going on?"

"I was putting stuff away in the attic and just felt along the walls. I found a crevice and that was in it." He paused, a question coming to his mind. "Did you know it was there?"

She shook her head. "I had no idea, but when we were renovating, we came upon hidden crevices just like you described. They were empty."

"Did you happen to find a hidden staircase?" He asked half in jest, but when she remained quiet, he looked up. "Did you?"

"Not a staircase. An iron ladder. No one else knows about it. It runs up to the attic from the basement."

"Show me, later. Right now, what can I help you with?"

"Nothing. Not right now anyway. By the way, where's your dad?" She had looked for him earlier as well and not found him.

"I have no idea. He was already up and gone when I woke this morning. But that's Dad. Give him something to track down and he won't let go." He turned as he heard his father's voice.

"Rory. Leah. There the two of you are." Riordan was in high spirits, earning him a suspicious glare from his son.

"Dad? Solved the mystery yet?"

Riordan grinned at the disgruntled tone of his son's voice. "Not yet. But I have found some interesting tidbits." He reached for a cup, finding Leah ahead of him, handing him his cup of tea. "Thank you, my dear. Now, what do we need to do to help?"

She shook her head. "What is it with you two? Always wanting to help. I managed quite well before you appeared."

"And that you did, my dear." Riordan caught the look on her face, the vulnerability she showed for a moment. "We're not saying that you can't continue, but we're here and we would like to help if you need us. If not, then we'll take ourselves out of the way."

She bit at her lip. "I'm sorry. I wasn't nice. It's all this that's going on. I'm not sleeping because of it. Fatigue makes my tongue sharp, Grams would tell me."

"Fatigue does funny things to our bodies. No offence." Riordan leaned against the granite countertop, his eyes on his cup. "Rory, you look like you're wanting to say something. Spit it out."

Rory broke out into laughter, knowing what his father was up to. "Spit it out? Dad. Really. Your language. Let you get away from Mom and your ability to put together decent sentences deteriorates." Riordan just grinned at his son, having gotten the reaction he was after. "And yes, I did find something. A crevice in the attic. And I hear there's a ladder running down from it as well."

"A ladder? Oh, now that sounds very interesting. I would like to take a look at it, if I may."

Leah sighed, staring around her kitchen, knowing she had much to do, but also wanting to be in on the search. "If you give me thirty minutes, I can show you."

"We'll do better than that. Tell us what you need us to do, and we'll help. Many hands make light work, you know." Riordan was off to wash his hands, back in no time, reaching for the tablecloths and napkins Leah had in her hands. "I can do that, at least I think I can."

She laughed at his nonsense. "I'm sure you can." She turned back to the counter, intent on the freshly-baked bread she needed to slice. "Rory? How are you at slicing bread?"

"Not bad, I guess."

An hour later, Riordan sat at Leah's desk, the maps spread out in front of him. "These are interesting. I would say these go back to your grandfather's time, just by the writing and the shore profile. It doesn't give much information as to why they would be hidden though. No "X" marking a treasure spot."

"I have never seen those, so I have no idea what they are for." Leah stood beside him, a finger tracing the shoreline on one of the maps. "This has changed so much over the years."

"That it has. That is what is likely throwing off our visitors."

"Dad, what are you saying?"

Riordan looked up, a grim look on his face. "I was at your local historical society and then your library this morning, Leah. I have a lot of information to sort through, but the general conception is that there are rumours of a fortune buried in this house, and that you know where it is and used it to renovate."

"What?" Her face paling, she stepped backwards, right into Rory who stood there. His arms encircled her, keeping her on her feet. "I used the life insurance Grams had socked away for me to do that. There was hers as well that I am using day to day until this starts paying for itself."

"That I understand. But the rumours are there. I am sure some of your guests have come just for that purpose." He stood, heading for the office door. "I need to look around your house more thoroughly, this time from a security standpoint. If you will let me."

"Sure. I guess. I never thought I'd be facing this." She stood still, Rory's arms around her as she watched Riordan start his search. "Can I help in any way?"

He turned to look at her, searching first her face and then his son's. "No, I don't think so. Rory, your task is to stick with her. If needed, I'll pull in Reilly or Redmond or the both. They're back home so they're available."

Leah paled even further. "You want to bring in more people?"

"Just my two brothers. At least he hasn't said Regan or Ryanne."

She groaned. "And they would be?"

"My sisters. They are a force to be reckoned with. They had the three of us boys shaking in our boots as kids."

Riordan gave a shout of laughter at that, his face alight with memories. "They could do that, son. How many times did we have to rescue you three boys from them?"

"Too many, and that was only because you raised us to be gentlemen."

Riordan continued to laugh as he moved away, his eyes and hands busy searching.

Leah leaned back against Rory, not realizing what she had done. "They are like that?"

"Not quite as bad as it sounds, but they are formidable." He hugged her tighter, his chin on the top of her head. "Now what do we need to do?"

"The garden. I have to gather the vegetables from there."

He reluctantly let her go, reaching for her hand as they walked towards the kitchen and the back door. "Do you have a basket then and a knife or scissors whatever it is you use?"

She pointed to the basket even as she tried to extract her hand. His hand tightened on hers as he took the basket and then led her out the door to the back yard, pausing for a moment to draw a deep breath. "This place is so relaxing."

"It certainly isn't." She studied his face for a moment. "Wait! You really mean that?"

"I do. Compared to the places I've been - places torn apart by drugs, wars, whatever - this is peaceful. We'll make it that way for you again, Leah, God willing. And that I have no doubt about. He does not want you to live in fear."

"I know He does. It's just hard to see at the moment." She stopped, her mouth dropping open as she stared at her garden. "Oh, no! What did they do?"

Rory stared as well, as the destruction wrought there. "Let's see what we can salvage. It may not be as bad as you think."

An hour later, he straightened up, looking around. They had managed to salvage about three quarters of the plants. The veggies that came from the destroyed plants had been sorted through and set aside.

"They are warning you. I pray it doesn't get worse than this.'

She looked around, thankful for his help. "I pray it doesn't. I can't afford to be buying all these veggies. I would have to dramatically change my menu. It will be bad enough in the winter buying them."

He searched her face and then spotted an old building, foundation really. "What's in that?"

"That? That an old carriage house. It's in ruins, though. Why?"

"Because if the foundation is good, we could work up a greenhouse for you, and you wouldn't have to buy veggies in the winter."

"I can't afford that."

He shook his head even as he pulled her towards the ruins. "You don't have to. I know someone who gives grants. This would be perfect, if I know him. And I do."

"Rory, you need to stop this. Please? Let me catch my breath." She stood at the entrance to the carriage house, looking over it, trying to see it from his point of view. "I'm not seeing what you mean."

Rory had been taking photos with his phone from many angles and held up a finger. He was in the process of sending them to his friend. "There. He has the photos. He'll let me know what he thinks. You have a pond behind you that could be used for hydroponics, which would help. He'll want to see it in person, that much I know."

"Rory, why?" She was almost in tears, hope springing up in her that just maybe she could make a go of the B&B.

"Why? Because you're special. And I want to do this for you." He searched her face before coming over and dropping a kiss on her cheek. He stood watching as her hand went to the spot, her mouth rounded. "I'm sorry. I shouldn't have done that."

"No, it's okay. I'm just surprised." She opened her mouth to comment further when his phone rang.

"It's Timothy. Let me talk to him for a moment." He raised the phone to his ear and before he could even speak, he could hear the excitement in his friend's voice. A relieved laugh escaped from him. "Timothy? Can you slow down a moment please? You think it would work? You do, huh. What's that? You want to come this way, you and Rachel? Sure. We could find a spot for you. A bed on the floor for her and a nail in the wall to hook your sweater on and hang you from. When? Tomorrow? Sure. Let me ask Leah." He turned, finding Leah staring at him, shock on her face. "Leah? He thinks it's a go. He just needs measurements.   He and his wife want to head this way tomorrow, if it's convenient."

She stared at him some more, her emotions in a whirl, not quite sure what to think. She watched for a moment, seeing him about to refuse, when her hand came out, her head nodding, her eyes flooding with grateful tears. "It's okay. Tell them to come. I have an empty room for tomorrow night that they can have, no charge."

"Timothy, it's okay. She has a room for you as well if you want to stay. You do, huh? We'll see you tomorrow. It's what, about a two hour drive, you think? What's that?   No, they're not here.   Not yet, anyway. Dad is but I'm not sure how long he'll be here. All right then, we'll see you in the morning." He pocketed his phone, his hands then reaching for Leah's. "He'll come and look, but won't do a thing if you say no. And it won't cost you anything. He runs a foundation now that does this for small businesses. He also runs a business that helps seniors stay in their own home until they can't any longer."

"How do you know him?" They had turned to walk back towards the house, stopping to gather the baskets from the garden. She gave a huge sigh. "Those men have made a lot of work for me. I'll need to deal with these today so they don't go bad."

Rory was about to speak when he heard his name called. "Mom? What are you going here?"

"Your father told me about a wonderful B&B and suggested that I come. Now, I know I shouldn't have. Your friend not likely will have a room for us."

Leah stared at the woman for a moment, finally realizing it was Rory's mother. "This is your mother, Rory?"

"Rory, you didn't introduce us. I'm Naomi. And yes, I'm this brat's mother." She reached to hug Leah, holding on for a little bit, feeling the younger woman's need just to be held by a mother.

"You didn't give me a chance, Mom." He shot a look at Leah, seeing a peaceful expression on her face. "I can bunk anywhere. You and Dad can have my room."

"I have an extra bedroom in my quarters, Naomi. I suggest you and Riordan use it." She turned to him, a mischievous look on her face. "How many more of your relatives and friends can I expect?"

Naomi looked between the two, seeing the slightly sheepish look on Rory's face. "He didn't, did he? Which one did he ask?"

"Someone named Timothy. He's coming to look at the old carriage house with the idea of making it into a greenhouse. Apparently that's possible."

"Timothy? And Rachel? Wonderful. Now young lady, let me help you with those. What on earth did you mean picking all those?"

"It wasn't planned." Rory shared a look with his father who had appeared. "Someone tried to destroy her garden, Dad."

Riordan slowly nodded. "I suspected that when I saw you with those baskets.

Show me, son." The two men walked off, leaving the women chatting as they headed for the kitchen.

The man watching from the trees swore, his curses disturbing the birds and insects surrounding him. This was not what he had planned. He had planned to scare her away, for her to abandon the house, and then he could search in peace. Instead, more people were arriving to help her. This could not go on. How did he drive her away? He turned, heavy footsteps trampling anything in his path as he headed for the bay and his boat.

Chapter 10

Leah stood for a moment in the attic doorway, looking around. She sighed. Rory had been up here, she knew that. He had tidied it all up and away for her. What was she to do with him, she wondered? She walked through the attic, stopping every once in a while to touch a piece of furniture, or a trunk. She paused, her head turning, feeling something off, before she was struck on the back of the head. She crumpled to the floor, the man standing over her, his eyes full of hatred on her, before he turned, hearing the sound of footsteps on the stairs. He faded away, the wall closing after him.

Rory's voice called for Leah before he appeared in the doorway. He hesitated for a moment, looking for her. Then with a cry, he sprang forward, his hands reaching for her even as he dropped to his knees. He gently felt her head, seeing the blood, before he scooped her into his arms, hurrying down the steps, his mother appearing at his call.

"Rory? What on earth?" Naomi's hands reached to check Leah as she lay against Rory's shoulder. "Here. Into the sunroom and to the couch there. Then find the first aid kit. I'll need warm water as well."

Rory was away to do his mother's bidding as she knelt beside Leah. "Oh, Leah. What did you go and do?"

Leah stirred, her head pounding. "I didn't do anything. Someone hit me."

"Someone hit you? I didn't see anyone else there." Rory stood, basin of warm water in his hand, waiting for his mother to move.

"No, you won't. The entrance to the ladder was behind me. Whoever this is has found it. We'll need to block it off." Pain laced her words.

"That we can do. Tell me exactly where it is and where to find wood. I'll make sure he doesn't get in again." Rory tamped down his anger, knowing it would not serve any purpose now.

She described where to find it, and then handing the basin to his mother, he was off to the garage, his father meeting him there.

"Rory?   What on earth are you doing?"

"Blocking off the ladder in the attic. Leah was just knocked out. That has to have been how he's been getting in and out."

Rory reached for the wood Rory had unearthed. "Let me help you. What time do Timothy and Rachel arrive?"

Rory glanced at his watch. "In about thirty minutes. This is not how I wanted them to meet Leah."

"No, I don't suspect that it was. How is she?"   Riordan's hand on his sons' shoulder kept him in place.

"Hurting, Dad, in more ways than one. Who does this? She doesn't deserve this."

"No one does, but that's what happens in life. You know that, son." He stood back, watching as Rory finished with the wood. "We'll need to take a look at that soon."

"I know we will. But until then, it stays this way. I won't have her hurt again."

Riordan smiled at the fierce look on his son's face. "She's gotten to you, hasn't she, son?" When Rory wouldn't answer, his father just hugged him. "She's the lady you've been looking for, son. Your mother and I can see that."

Rory finally nodded. "She may be, Dad. But that's something I have to discuss with her."

"And rightly so. Now, let's get this put away. We'll look at this another day, when we're on our own. Is Timothy staying overnight?"

"I have no idea. She's offered the empty room to them." He groaned. "She was going to put it to rights when she was done up here, she said." He ran for the stairs, heading for the room Leah had designated. "And she's got it done. When did she have time for that?"

"She likely did it first thing, son, when the guests left. That's her style." He paused for a moment, his eyes on the far wall. "And what is this?"

Rory followed his line of sight before he reached for the envelope stuck to the wall with a piece of tape. "This is not good. And we have no choice. We have to give it to her."

"We do. It's addressed to her."

Leah was sitting up on the couch, an ice pack on the back of her head when the two men found her. Naomi had headed for the kitchen, intent on finding some painkillers and water for the younger woman.

"Leah, we found this on a wall upstairs."

She grimaced as she moved, Rory sitting down quickly beside her. "What is it?"

"An envelope with your name on it. We didn't open it."

"Go ahead. It can't be that personal." She ignored the sound of voices and of Riordan greeting them. "Well?"

Rory stared at it, before his eyes raised to hers. "It warns you to turn over the treasure or worse things will happen to you."

She snorted, bringing his eyes back to her face. "I highly doubt there can be much more than they can do." She looked up at him, seeing the look on his face. "You think there is."

"There always is. Without knowing where the treasure is or even what it is, we can't do what they say. I know you're committed to following through on the hunt."

"You've got that right." She shoved aside his hand, stood, wobbling for a moment before she headed for the kitchen, startling Naomi as she reached for a bottle of water. "Thanks, Naomi. I'll just take them without water." She reached for the pain killers. "I know. You don't want me moving around. The headache will disappear, eventually, and there are things I need to do." She headed for the back stairs, disappearing from sight as Riordan returned with a younger couple.

"Where's Leah?" He didn't see her and turned to head for the sunroom, stopping at his wife's laughter.

"She's not there, love. She headed up the stairs."

"Oh. Send Rory after her. She needs to meet Timothy and Rachel."

Naomi shook her head. "Just take them out to the carriage house, or Timothy at any rate. Rachel can stay and visit with me and with Leah when she eventually returns."

Leah stood for a moment at the back door, watching as the men moved around the carriage house. Naomi had disappeared and so had the basket for her garden. That must be where she is, Leah thought, before she headed to her office. She had paperwork that needed to be done and a bank deposit to make. She headed for town, not thinking to leave a note, causing great concern in her wake until she returned a couple of hours later.

Rory met her in the kitchen, a frown on his face. "Leah?"

She jumped, then reached for her head. "Rory? Are you always so quiet?"

"I didn't think I was that quiet. Where were you? I was worried."

She studied his face, seeing the concern there, and realized what he would have thought. "I'm sorry. I had to do a bank deposit." She sighed. "I'm not used to having to tell people where I am."

"That's okay. It's just we need to talk to you about the carriage house. Do you have some time?"

She glanced at the clock. "I don't need to start the tea for another hour or so. Let me change my shoes and I'll meet you."

She came back to find him standing here, his eyes on the floor as he leaned against the wall. He looked up at her, his heart on his face without him knowing it, causing her to draw in her breath sharply. He grinned at her and reached for her hand.

"Timothy is all excited about this. He sees great potential in the building."

"He does? Well, I don't know what to say." She started for the door, stopping as he reached for her hand. "Rory?"

"I'm excited about this. But keep in mind. This is your property. We have no right to agree to do anything without your input. If you hesitate or say no, that will be all it takes. Timothy will leave the plans he's drawing up for you and then walk away."

"Just like that?"

"Just like that. He and Rachel have been through a lot and learned to really trust God in a way few don't. Some day I'll tell you their story. Just so you know, his father was a police officer. Rachel's brother is a private investigator and works at times for his brother-in-law's security firm."

"They do? I mean, they are? I don't know what I mean. This has me flustered."

"Really? You'd never know." He grinned at her discomfort before he hugged her and then led her by the hand towards the ruins. "Timothy's really running with this. He says he can use the foundation almost as it is, building up from it for the greenhouse, using the basement as the guts of it as he puts it and for storage."

"Wow! He's done that all ready?" Leah stared at the young man walking towards them, a beautiful woman beside him.

"They don't bite." Rory grinned at the frown she threw him.

She stood talking for a while with the three, then excused herself, knowing she was needed in the kitchen and feeling overwhelmed. Rachel watched her go, then turned to Rory.

"Are you sure she's ready for this, Rory?"

He hesitated. "I think so. She's not used to people helping her. She's had to do so much on her own for so many years."

He turned as he heard Timothy muttering something and reached to stop his hand from picking up the envelope.

"Rory?" Timothy's voice held more than a question. It held a warning.

"I know. I know. It's the second one I've found today."

"The second one? What have you gotten involved in?"

"A treasure hunt, I'm told, but Leah doesn't think there is any treasure. Just rumours."

"And with her renovating the house, they think she's found it and has been using it. Is that what you're saying?"

"Exactly. Let's see what this says. It is addressed to me. Now, how did that come about?"

Rachel shook her head. "You two figure it out. I had enough adventures to last a lifetime. I'm going to find Leah and see what I can do to help." She was off before the men could react.

Rory stared at the envelope before he opened it, finding only a picture of himself. "This isn't from here."

"No, it's from the park near your home. Isn't that the one on your website?"

"It is. Someone has downloaded it and printed it. Now why?"

"A warning, I would say. Somehow, they've connected you to the website and now that makes you a target. They think you're here to protect her."

"That wasn't my plan or intentions when I landed here. God sent me this way. Now I'm here, I know why. I can't walk away and leave her to face this on her own."

"None of us would. Not the men I'm friends with. Your family will back you no matter what you do. And I know a team that will come in if needed."

"I know you do. And yes, they will." Rory stuffed the envelope into his pocket.

"Now about your plans? What else do you need to do for them?"

"I have all the measurements I need. I can do a provisional plan today and print it off for her to look at. She can make any changes she wants to it, as long as it will work. And I can't see her many too many demands."

"No, I can't see her doing that. So, other than the grants, what are you involved with?" The two men were lost in conversation, not seeing the man patrolling along the back fence, intent on what they were doing.

Leah found them shortly afterwards, her hand on Rory's arm stopping them. "Rory. Timothy. Come. We have lunch ready for us. Set aside your plans and we'll eat. Then we can talk some more." She frowned as she saw the dust rising from the back of the yard and then sighed. The men had been too engrossed in their conversation to see that man. It was useless now to say anything, she knew. He would be long gone. She had seen him before and thought him to be a stranger who had lost his way. Now she wasn't so sure.

Rory caught her hand in his as they walked back towards the house, noting that for once she didn't try to pull away from him, instead moving closer to him. Timothy eyed them, intending on talking to Rachel when he had a moment, to get her thoughts on Leah. He sighed, knowing what he was up to and asking forgiveness for his doubt. He knew God had placed these two in the same spot for a reason.

Leah was content, but not content, and she snorted to herself. She really had no idea what she meant and she could not explain it easily. Rory made her feel safe, even with what was going on, and she refused to depend on anyone. That was a given, she thought.

Rory pulled her to a stop, nodding as Timothy pointed to himself and then the house. He waited for a moment before he looked down at Leah, who was staring at the house, a mutinous look on her face.

"Leah? Talk to me. If you want all this to stop, just say the word." His words were quiet and resigned.

She shook her head, and he saw for the first time the tears in her eyes. "It's not you or Timothy or your dad or your mom. It's me. I am having such a hard time with this and I shouldn't. I know that."

"Talk to me." He drew her to a bench under an apple tree, seating her and then when he had seated himself, wrapping an arm around her.

"It's me.   I know it has to be. Whoever this is is after me. You being here has placed yourself in danger. I don't want that."

"Leah, my love, listen to me. I live for danger. It's been my life for so long. That's what I do. God has put me here. Don't think anything different. If I didn't feel that and feel that I was placed here to keep you safe, then I would walk away.   That's a given. Now. There's something else. What is it?"

She sighed, her head going to his shoulder without any thought on her part that it was an odd movement for her to make. "It's all this talk about treasure. I saw a man at the back of the yard when I came to get you. He's been around before and no, I can't describe him. And no, I don't want a dog. I can't take that responsibility, not when I have paying guests."

"That doesn't leave you many options, does it? We can put up security cameras at the back, where it won't be intrusive to your guests. They don't go back there. You've made that clear that the back yard is out of bounds."

"It is. I need somewhere I can retreat to. I used to retreat to the front porch, but can't any more."

"I see that. So where does that leave us?"

"I'm sorry, I'm not sure what you mean. Where does that leave us? Is there an us?" She twisted her head to stare at him.

"I would like there to be, but I won't pressure you in any way, shape or form. We need to get to know one another." He looked down at her, then raised his eyes to the horizon. "I'm thinking I like this town too much to move on."

"But, Rory? Your work? Don't you work for your Dad?"

"I did, but I don't have to. I can find something else to do."

She shook her head. "You can't do that. Not for me. It's part of who you are. I can see that."

"I can work from here. A lot of what we do is over the internet anyway. I don't have to be the one going overseas or out to rescue. In fact, Dad and I had talked about that. He wanted to use me more in the office and doing research. He said that was where I was best suited. He just wanted me to gain experience in the field."

"And can you do that from here?" She was seeking, she knew, for reassurance that he wasn't just saying that.

"I can. The office is only a couple of hours away. I can go in if I really need to. Mom and Dad have an apartment in their basement I've been using. We can leave it set up just for that." He finally rose, drawing her to her feet. "We'll talk more later. I found another envelope, this time with a picture of me. No warning. Nothing written. Let's leave it for now and go see if they've left us any lunch."

"That I wouldn't count on. Your mom said Timothy had a big appetite as does your Dad."

Rory began to laugh. "That they do, but I can guarantee she'll have put aside food for us."

She nodded, then spoke. "Thank you, Rory. Your words and offer to stay mean a lot to me."

Chapter 11

Raising up in the early morning hours, Rory looked around, trying to determine what had awakened him. He rose, dressed and headed for the door in his room that led to the back yard. He opened it cautiously, squinting in the dim light before he returned to his dresser and felt for his flashlight. He slipped out the door, letting his eyes become accustomed to the darkness and then stepped off the porch, his feet sinking into the dew-drenched grass. He walked the perimeter of the house and then headed for the perimeter of the yard, his eyes searching for whatever it was that had awakened him. He paused for a moment, his head turned as he listened, then headed for the back of the yard, knowing that was where the noise was coming from.

He paused once more, his eyes on the men digging around the foundation of the carriage house. That's what had awakened him, he knew. He crept closer, his feet silent on the grass, until he stood, back to the stone foundation, and waited. He listened to the quiet words, not able to distinguish any. He moved closer, not seeing the man watching him.

Rory turned as he heard a noise behind him, but not before the knife slashed towards him, catching him on the ribs and slicing through the flesh and muscle. Rory gave a choked cry, his hand going to the area before he sank to the ground, the man's foot catching him in the head. His vision darkened as he saw booted feet moving past him and then darkness claimed him.

Leah arose in the early morning hours as had become her custom, tying on her apron as she hummed softly to herself, knowing Rory would be in the kitchen waiting for her. Surprised not to see him, she shrugged and went about preparing the breakfast foods she provided for her guests. Two hours later, she stood back, listening to the conversations in the dining room as the guests helped themselves from the buffet. She nodded at Timothy and Rachel and then returned to the kitchen, to find Naomi already there, working to clear up the mess that had been left.

"You don't have to do that, Naomi." Leah greeted her with a smile.

Naomi smiled. "I know I don't but I want to. What do we have on the agenda for today? I like this work, you know. Maybe I should retire and come work for you."

"You'd do that?" At Naomi's nod, Leah reached to hug her. "Thank you. Now, where's Rory? Have you seen him? He didn't show up this morning to help."

"He didn't? He wasn't in his room. Riordan went looking for him."

A sudden rattle at the back door startled them before Leah sprang to open it, standing back, a hand to her mouth as she saw Riordan staggering in, Rory in his arms. Naomi sprang to help, running to turn down the bedding in Rory's room. Leah scrambled to find bandages and the first aid kit, a basin of water and cloths, not quite sure what was needed, but seeing the blood on Rory's side, knowing he had been hurt.

"Riordan?" Leah moved to stand beside him. "What happened?"

"I don't know. I found him down by the carriage house. It looks as if he approached it sometime overnight. There's evidence of new digging there."

Naomi looked up. "It's bad, Riordan. I can't stitch it. We need medical help." Her gaze shot to Leah. "Is there a doctor here as a guest?"

"No, I don't think so." Leah's voice died away. "Wait. There is. He's retired from practice he said. Let me see if he's still here." She was away in a flash, returning with a white-haired gentleman, who gently moved Naomi to one side.

"This is Dr. Jones. He's on vacation."

"What happened?" He spoke, his voice professional and quiet, even as his hands worked to assess Rory. "He's been stabbed. I would say at least three hours or more ago. Where did you find him?"

"He was outside. I went looking for him. He's my son."

Dr. Jones shot Riordan a quick look. "Your son? Any health issues? Allergies? I see a scar below this. He's been hurt before? And not that long ago."

"No health issues. No allergies. Yes, he was hurt. He was shot at and it just grazed him."

"Shot? Here?"

"No. It was overseas, about four months ago." Riordan heard Leah's indrawn breath and turned to pull her close to him, his arm steady around him. "He had healed completely from that, he was told."

"He has. Whoever sewed him up did a nice job. The scar will eventually fade. Now, about this." He turned to Naomi, watching her closely. "I'll need help. I can go get my wife."

Naomi shook her head. "He's my son. I will help. What do I need to do?"

"Young lady, do you have any disinfectant?"

"I do." Leah ran for her supplies and returned. "I have this. It was recommended by my own doctor to have on hand."

"Perfect. Here, wash your hands with this. I'm sorry. I didn't get your name."

Naomi reached for the bottle. "It's Naomi. I'll be right back. What else do you need?"

"This kit is well supplied. Your doctor look after it?" Dr. Jones shot another look at Leah.

"He did.   He put in everything he would want in it, including those sutures and needles. Are they okay to use?"

"Absolutely. You're not going to faint on me, are you, as we work on your young man? If you are, leave."

She stared at him before shaking her head. "No, I won't faint." Riordan's arm tightened on her. She turned. "We need to let Timothy and Rachel know."

"We will. Once we know that Rory is okay. Dr. Jones, I think he's been kicked or hit as well in the head."

"I see that. Let's get him stitched up and I'll take a look at that. I don't think it was too hard, though. There doesn't seem to be too much of a mark."

Dr. Jones finally stood back, his eyes assessing first Rory, then Leah. He frowned. "You have a headache, young lady. What happened to you?"

She sighed. "I was knocked out yesterday morning. Yes, I have a headache but nothing that I can't handle."

He swung a chair around. "Sit. Let me assess you. No, sit. It won't hurt. I don't hurt pretty young ladies." He grinned as she stared at him for a moment before she sat, wincing slightly as his fingers probed the sore spot. "You've a lump there. Ice it. Take painkillers as you want." He stepped towards the door before he turned back. "I'm off for a walk with my wife. I won't disappoint her in that. She's always been first in my life. I'll stop in again when I'm back. If you have any concerns, Leah, you have my phone number. Just call me." He was gone before their thanks could be uttered.

Riordan drew Leah from the room, meeting Timothy and Rachel standing outside the door.

"How is he?" Timothy watched Riordan intently.

"He was stabbed, Timothy, and then kicked in the head, Dr. Jones said. Out by the carriage house. There's fresh digging there as well." Riordan ushered them away from the door and towards the kitchen. "Rachel? How long can you two stay?"

"For a couple of days, I think. Timothy?"

"I'll call Dad and you can call Gideon. They'll look after what we were planning on doing. Is there room for us to stay?"

Leah nodded, tears of relief sparkling in her eyes for a moment. "Thank you. I have another spare room in my quarters. I need the room you're in tonight for a guest. Feel free to move to the bedroom beside Naomi and Riordan." She sank to a stool, her head cradled in her hands for a moment before she looked up. "This will not stop me. It will not close the B&B. Riordan, I'm sorry. I'm so sorry."

"Sorry? For what?" He sat down beside her, his hands reaching for hers just as he would for one of his daughters'. "For Rory getting hurt? That's Rory. If he heard something, he would have gone to investigate. He wouldn't have worried you over that. He'll recover. You heard Dr. Jones. The wound wasn't deep. He's had a lot worse."

"He has? But not on my account. I can't let him continue to investigate." She looked up, startled as the three with her began to laugh.

"That's not happening, Leah. He'll continue, whether you let him or not. He won't rest until he's solved whatever it is that's going on. If you have any names you need investigated, let me know. I have a friend who does that." Timothy just shook his head at her before he looked around. "Now, we need to go over your plans, but I suspect you have work to do first. Hand me an apron and I'll get started on the dishes. Rachel?"

"An apron for me as well and I'll look after the food. Riordan?"

He grinned as he stood before dropping a kiss on Leah's head and hugging her, treating her like his own. "Lead me to a vacuum or broom or whatever it is you use to clean up. I'm an expert at that."

Leah sat, motioning to where everything was kept, her eyes sparkling once more with unshed tears. She had not felt so comforted and loved, not since her Grams left her the year, not two years now, she thought. Has it been that long already, Grams? Thank you, Lord, for sending these people to me. Heal Rory please, dear Lord.

She tiptoed into the room, causing Naomi's head to raise from where she had seated herself near the window. Naomi watched as Leah dropped to her knees beside the bed, her hand reaching for Rory's, and then the other hand to his face, before her head dropped to their hands and her shoulders shook. Naomi didn't move, didn't disturb the younger woman, knowing she needed to heal, and this was one part of that. Leah finally raised her head, her hand swiping at her cheeks, before she rose and walked from the bedroom, determination in her steps and stance. Now what is she up to, dear Lord? Naomi's whispered question echoed through the room. She could tell Leah had made a decision and worried that she would place herself in danger.

Rory stirred, a hand going to his head before his ribs. His eyes flickered open and he stared at the ceiling, a frown in place. He turned his head, searching for Leah, knowing she had been there. He had felt her tears and her whispered prayer but hadn't been able to rouse himself enough. He turned his head again as he heard movement and his mother sat on the edge of the bed.

"Mom? What happened? Where's Leah?"

"You went and got yourself into trouble. You've been stabbed and hit over the head. We had a doctor in to see you. Leah just left. I can get her for you." Her troubled eyes watched her son closely.

"No, that's okay, Mom. I just thought I heard her praying."

"You did. She was here, didn't speak to me, just knelt beside you and then rose and walked away."

"Don't let her do anything stupid, okay Mom?" Rory's eyes slid shut and he slept.

"I won't, son. I won't let your lady hurt herself, not if I can help it. Sleep now. Heal quickly. She needs you."

Riordan stood in the doorway, finally walking over to the bed and reaching for his wife's hand. "He's been awake?"

"He has. His first thought was for Leah. Is she the one?"

"Is she the one? The one we've prayed for since he was born?" At her nod, Riordan paused to think. "I would say she is. They suit each other so well. But only God knows if they are meant to be a couple. All we can do is pray for them."

Leah stood listening to them before she spoke, startling them and causing them to turn to face her. "You did that?"

"Did what, love?" Naomi moved to hug her, then stood back, her eyes on Leah's face, her arms still around her.

"You prayed for his wife, even as a child you prayed for that?" At their nod, she sighed. "My parents and grandparents did that too. One of the last things Grams did was to pray for my life mate. Thank you." She hesitated. "But I can't let him continue to search."

"You might as well tell the sun not to shine. As soon as he's up and about, he'll be working. And if I know him, he'll be doing that before he's up. He has a laptop he'll use." Riordan reached to hug her as well. "Now, tell us what you need to do. If there's nothing I can help with, I'm taking Timothy and walking down to the bay. It's the path from the back of the yard?"

"It is. But please be careful. I don't want anyone else hurt."

Chapter 12

A week later, Rory was on his feet, moving carefully at times, but back to trying to protect Leah as best he could. She was frustrated with him, he knew, but he could do nothing else. His parents had left for their own home. Before he had left, his father talked to Rory, telling him that they had not been able to find any evidence of the assault. The police had been out but could offer little assistance. Riordan had watched as Rory snorted and replied that of course they couldn't. Rory had his own thoughts on that.

Sitting at Leah's desk, his laptop in front of him, Rory searched through his messages. He finally rose, heading to get his work phone, the one he had stuck away all those week ago. He dreaded turning it on, knowing the message box would be full, and he would have way too many text messages. He sat back down in the chair in the office, his eyes on his phone, his thoughts on Leah, who had insisted he leave her to work in peace. He was hovering, he knew, but couldn't help himself. He offered a quick prayer for strength, peace and guidance before he powered up the phone and began a systematic process of working through the messages. Most he forwarded on to the office, knowing they would be the ones to deal with them before he changed his voice mail greeting, asking that all parties contact the office number.

His text messages were numerous. He paused at a couple, not quite sure what they were about, and made note to investigate the numbers. The last message, sent the day he was hurt, sent chills down his spine. He rose, his intent to find Leah, when he paused and sat back down. There was something off about the message and he needed Reilly's help on that. He forwarded it on, knowing it would be taken care of.

He finally rose and stretched, feeling the pull of the wound and the sutures. He frowned. Riordan had told them they have found no evidence of any more digging going on, but he knew what he saw. He headed through the kitchen, looking for Leah, but not seeing her. Please, let her be safe, Lord.

He paused near the carriage house, seeing the piles of lumber already inside. Timothy had wasted no time in securing an architect, having Leah approve of the plans and then hiring a contractor. Her choice had been to hire local, stating that was her policy, if at all possible. He had agreed, finding someone who was willing to start work. Timothy had told him privately that the town was pulling for Leah to make a go of the B&B, as it brought in more revenue for them all.

Leah watched Rory for a moment before she approached him, clearing her throat to alert him.

He turned, a huge grin on his face. "Leah! I was looking for you!"

"You were? And why would that be?"

"I just wanted to know where you were and that you were safe. Here, set your basket of goodies down for a moment. I'm just in the process of heading towards where I saw the men digging. Dad said the police found no evidence of that."

Leah snorted. "Not with the one they sent. He only does the bare minimum. He needs to retire and won't." She suddenly grinned at him. "You could join the force and take over his job."

Rory shook his head, a look of pretend horror crossing his face. "Not for me, thank you very much." He stood for a moment, gauging his distance and then walked towards the foundation. "It was right about here." He pointed to the ground. "And they said they couldn't find anything. This is where it was. I'm sure of that. Look, you can see freshly turned earth. Now why didn't anyone else see that?"

"Your dad did." When Rory looked up at her from where he had crouched down, she nodded. "He saw that and dug into it. He didn't go down too far, but he said it was where they were digging. It's the only spot that was disturbed."

"Thanks, Leah. That helps." Rory stood and then moved to stand beside her. "What else did Dad have to say?"

"Not a lot, other than I was to keep you out of trouble." She grinned. "He did clarify that. If I could, was how he put it."

Rory choked on his laughter. "That would be Dad. Now, have you received any more strange mail? Any parcels? Any concerning phone calls?"

"None. That surprises me. I think it will become worse though once the men start working on the greenhouse. Just how did Timothy get it started so soon?"

"Prayer. Determination. He doesn't sit back if something needs to be done."

"He certainly doesn't. You say his father is a retired officer?"

"Ben? He is, but you can't talk to him." At her look of outrage, he smirked. "They're away on vacation and won't be back for a month."

"Well, then I guess it's you and I. What have you discovered?"

He reached to take her basket from her hand and then, arm around her shoulders, turned her towards the house. "I had a disturbing message on my work phone. That I've sent on to one of my brothers to look at." He sighed. "I know. You want to know what it said."

"If I could. If it's personal, then no."

"It's only personal in that I was warned to leave here. That what I received is mild to what I could have." He watched as her face shadowed. "No, no worrying."

"And you expect me just to set that aside? Rory! You were hurt because of me!"

Rory shook his head. "No, I don't think so. I think there is something else going on. I just can't pin it down. Dad said when he and Timothy walked the beach, they didn't find anything out of the ordinary." He opened the door, waited for her to enter, before he came through, setting the basket on the counter and starting to unload it.

"I didn't think they would. Whoever this is has been too careful." She paused, her hands full of tomatoes, before she dropped them into a sinkful of water. "We have never gone down the ladder and I think we need to."

"At some point, we will. Not right now."

She shrugged, her thoughts going to what she had been faced with, and then she sighed. "Rory. I just can't go on. This B&B isn't worth it. Not when they tried to kill you."

He had been closely watching her. "Don't give up your dream. Not for me. Not for anyone."

"But I can't have anyone else hurt. No one's life is worth that." She turned from the sink, reaching for a towel to dry her hands before throwing it on the counter. She stalked away from him, heading for the dining room. She needed to work in there, but her heart wasn't in it any more. Lord, I give up. I can't do this.

Rory had moved to stand in the doorway, his eyes following her, seeing her defeat. He spun. There had to be something he could do to relieve her stress and her anxiety. His phone vibrated, disturbing him. He pulled it out with a frown. It was his father.

"Dad?"

"Rory?" His father's voice sounded rushed and he could hear the sound of traffic. "I'm on my way back there. Stay close to Leah. Don't let her out of your sight. I'll be there in about thirty minutes."

"Dad? Why?" Rory was puzzled. His father had been scheduled to fly overseas but obviously hadn't.

"Because you have both been threatened. That message you sent on? The one you couldn't make sense of? Reilly found it to be cryptic and decoded it. It is a direct threat. Stay safe, son." The connection dropped.

Rory stared at his phone for a moment before he pocketed it. Just how do I do that, Lord? How do I keep this lady safe? She's ready to walk away from her dream.

"Rory?" Her voice startled him and he looked up at her even as he walked towards her. "Rory? What is going on now? You look angry."

"Frustrated would be a better word. Dad's on his way back. I told you about the message I sent on, didn't I?" At her nod, he reached to draw her to him. "Dad said Reilly decoded it. It was a warning."

"And I have brought more danger to you, haven't I?" She struggled to release herself from his arms.

As he heard the front door opening and closing, Rory drew her back into her own quarters and then to the sunroom. "You were threatened. Dad was to be overseas but cancelled to come here."

"He can't do that. He can't just drop everything to come to my rescue."

"He can. He has. To him, you're family. That's all that matters." Rory watched as the warring emotions flickered across her face. "Leah? Talk to me. Don't shut me out."

"What do you want me to say? That you need to leave? That you've been in danger since I met you? That I don't want you hurt?" Her voice dropped to a mere whisper. "And that I don't want you to leave." She turned, her arms wrapped around herself and sent to stand near the fireplace, her eyes on the empty hearth.

Rory drew a deep breath and approached her. "Leah? Are you saying what I think you're saying?" When she refused to look at him, his hand gently raised her chin. "Because if you are, then I am trying to say the same thing. Even though we haven't known each other for years, you are the only one for me."

She raised her eyes, searching his face. "It can't be, Rory. We need more time to get to know one another, don't we?"

"Danger does that. It can cement a friendship or tear it apart. With us, it's cemented our friendship and led to something else, has it not?" He paused, stepping back. "I won't say anything more. Come find me when you're ready to talk." He walked away, leaving her staring after him, a hand to her mouth, tears sparkling in her eyes.

She knew she needed to pray this through once more, had been praying for the attraction to disappear. Obviously, God didn't mean that to happen, or did He? She sighed, her hand dropping to the mantle and rubbing along the wood. What do I do, Lord? If he stays, he's likely to be hurt.

Rory stood for a moment, his head down, mixed emotions in his mind, before he headed to the dining room to finish setting the tables and arranging the dishes and plates on the buffet table. He glanced at the huge grandfather clock and noted it was now mid-afternoon. He wouldn't be going back to his work, not yet, he knew. He headed for the kitchen, stopping mid-step as he heard a sound and turned, trying to determine just where it was and unable to. He frowned as he stared at the wall in the hallway. There was something or someone behind there, he was sure. He would need to find those blueprints again.

Riordan tracked Leah down, finding her sitting in the sunroom, her eyes on her Bible. She looked up and smiled, but he could see the smile didn't reach her eyes, and the stress and fatigue lined her face.

"Riordan? Rory said you gave up a trip overseas. You shouldn't have."

Riordan smiled as he sat down beside her on the couch. "I had to, Leah. You and Rory are too important for me to leave when you're in danger."

She sighed. "Yes. That. The danger. Rory needs to leave."

"He won't." Riordan shook his head. "There is no way he'll walk away from you. Not ever."

"He has to." She went to rise, but his hand on his arm stopped her.

He had heard Rory's footsteps approaching and heard when they stopped. "You're too important to him, Leah. He doesn't walk away from his family or his friends. That's his character."

She nodded. "I know and he should. He'll be killed if he stays here." He could barely hear her whispered voice. "I couldn't live with myself if he is."

He looked over his shoulder and nodded at Rory. "Listen, I need to talk to both of you. Is this a good time?"

She glanced at her watch. "No, not really. I have to put out the buffet. That takes a bit and then I mingle with my guests. Tonight, maybe?"

"It will be tonight, Leah. I can't leave it for another day." Riordan rose and helped her to stand, reaching to hug her, and then sending her on her way, watching as she stopped beside Rory for a moment, her face raised to study him.

"Rory?"

His father's quiet voice brought his attention back to the room and he walked towards his father. "Dad? I found the spot where the men were digging. I also heard someone moving behind the wall in the hallway. How many secret passages are there that she doesn't know about?"

"There may only be a couple. We'll need to look into that." Riordan studied his son closely but chose not to say anything. "Show me where you think they were digging?   Is it different from the one I found?"

Chapter 13

Shaking her head, Leah stared at Riordan before her eyes moved to Rory, who was watching his father intently. "They can't do that, can they? Threaten us? Can't we charge them or something?"

"If we knew who they were, then yes, we could. Unfortunately, the phone number the text came from isn't working. It was likely a pay as you go phone that they've tossed." Riordan paced, his hands locked together behind his back. "What we have to do is come up with a plan to keep you two safe."

"And that doesn't mean bringing in strangers to Leah, now does it, Dad?" Rory knew how his father thought in these situations and was aware he had already looked into that.

"If I have to, I will." He held up a hand at Leah's protest. "I won't, Leah, not unless you two agree to that, or the situation comes to the point we don't have any choice."

"Then pray it never comes to that. I have enough to deal with, strangers around all the time." She spun and almost ran from the kitchen. They heard a door close quietly in the distance.

"She's adamant about that, Dad." Rory moved to the kitchen doorway, his eyes down the hallway. "She doesn't like a lot of fuss and bother about herself."

"I know that, Rory. Don't you think I can read her?" Riordan was frustrated, knowing he wanted to protect the two, but not able to.

"I know you can, Dad. All I'm saying is that right now, it's not a go. Don't bring anyone in." He turned to his father. "And do me a favour? Take that trip overseas that you need to. It won't help either one of us if you don't."

Riordan was silent for a moment before he nodded. "All right. I'll leave in the morning. But it's only for a couple of days."

"Thanks, Dad. That's what we want you to do." He paused, his eyes on his father's face, reading something there.

"You've gone and done something, haven't you?"

"No, just set some plans ready if we need them."

Rory shook his head. "Please, Dad?" He grinned. "I never thought I'd be the one begging you not to step in."

Riordan laughed as he reached to hug his son. "And I never thought I'd be having to plan to keep you safe. You're in the eye of the storm right now, you do realize that? That this is far from over?"

Rory nodded soberly. "I know, Dad. I don't like it. I don't want Leah hurt."

"It's like that, is it? I'm glad. She completes you."

"She does, does she?" Rory stepped away from his father as he heard footsteps walking their way.

Leah appeared in the doorway. "I'm sorry, Riordan. You're right to be concerned about Rory's safety. I should listen to what you are saying, and I didn't. What do we need to do?"

Riordan shook his head at them. "Yes, you do need to listen. This is what we planned, ready to set in place if we need to." He rapidly went through the plan, seeing Leah's look change from uncertainty to fear to determination, Rory's face remaining passive, but Riordan knew Rory was not happy.

"Are you in agreement with this, Leah?"

"I guess." She shrugged, not having ever thought she'd be danger. "When would you put this into place?"

"If I receive a direct threat that is consistent and with enough information for us to determine who or what is behind it. Even if we're not able to, if the threat is valid enough, we step in. We work with your local police in this."

She snorted. "Don't try that. They've made it clear they think I'm making everything up."

Rory spoke up. "They know better now, Leah. I had to file a report on my injury." He held up a hand as she protested. "It's necessary, Leah. I had no choice. We can't ignore the fact that something happened."

She sighed. "I know. I just wish you had talked to me first. Who did you report it to?"

"The chief himself. He's keeping it under wraps for now. I know him from years ago. He's confident that we can look after you, but will aid us if we ask."

"You know him? Wow! That's something." Leah looked at Riordan and then walked away, an unreadable look on her face.

"Is she in agreement or not?" Riordan looked over at his son, to find him watching the hall where Leah had disappeared.

"She says she is."

"But you're not sure on that?" Riordan pushed Rory to acknowledge that fact.

"I really don't know, Dad. She can be hard to read at times. This is one of them. I'll talk to her." Rory turned to his father. "Now, I know you have the plans all written down. Leave them with us. You need to be on your way. You were to be at that meeting this morning."

"I'm on my way. A friend is flying in here to pick me up and take me there."

"A friend? Well, I guess that's good." He hugged his father, who mentioned that Rory and Leah had better stay safe until he got back in a week. "We'll do our best, Dad. That's all we can do."

"I know, son. Call one of your brothers if you need help. Ryanne mentioned she would like to come here for a day or so. She's tired, Rory, and needs a break."

Rory sighed to himself. "I'll talk to Leah and see if there's a room available. I won't make any promises to Ryanne." He really didn't need his younger sister showing up.

"Thanks, son. I know it's not what you want, but she really does need a break. She's hurting over that last assignment, just like you are."

Rory nodded. "I know, Dad. We took the brunt of that, not getting there in time. I'll call her later."

With a wave, Riordan was gone. Rory stood for a moment, his eyes on the painting across from him before he frowned and walked towards it. Now, this is odd. He reached to lift it down as Leah came towards him.

"Rory, your father's gone?"

"He is. Leah, this painting? Has it always been here?"

She looked over his shoulder as he set it on the kitchen table. "It has. I have no idea who the artist is. I asked Grams one day and she didn't know either. Just said it was given to Gramps' Dad one time. So it is old. Why?"

"Because there's something odd about it." He flipped it over as he spoke. "Here, let's move the paper away a bit. It's really fragile and already disintegrating." He paused as his finger felt the back of the painting. "There's something here, Leah."

"Then by all means, let's move the paper away. It's not like we can save it." She ripped off the remaining paper, revealing an oilskin pouch. "Now, what is this, I wonder?"

Rory's hand stopped her. "Go, get your camera. We take pictures and then videotape us opening it. I just don't like the feeling I'm getting."

She stared at him for a moment before she was running for her camera and then back towards him. "Here. You take the still photos. I'll video tape it."

He nodded as he moved to take photos of the package. "Here. Your turn." He grinned as she shook her finger at him before she took the camera.

"What do you want me to do?"

"Start it and then aim it at the packet. This is going to be hard to open. Wait! Do you have thin knife that's sharp?"

She nodded, retrieving one from a drawer. "Here. This should do it. It's the knife Gramps used for filleting his fish."

"That will work. Thanks." He carefully worked the knife among the folds, gently opening the package and revealing its contents. Reaching for the camera, he took multiple pictures before he set the camera aside. "Now, what do we have here?"

Leah watched closely as Rory spread out the oilskin. "It's a map?"

"That's what it looks like. I have no idea where or what."

She leaned closer to him, her arm brushing against his. "That's the bay we went to. It's changed some but I recognize some of the landmarks. Those rocks there? The ones that look like a ship? They are still there."

Rory was puzzled. "I don't see any markings to indicate what it means. Do you?" He watched her as she shook her head, her hair swinging freely around her face.

"No, but there has to be a reason it was hidden." She reached for it, turning it over, pausing as she saw faded writing on it. "What's this, Rory?"

He squinted, not sure what was written there. "I don't know. But I know someone who could help. It means a trip home though."

"Really? When would you go?"

"What day can you swing it to have someone cover for you?" He watched as she stared at him for a moment, then thought through what he asked.

"Tomorrow. Lisa offered to cover for me if I needed a day. She's usually off on Tuesdays."

"Call her and ask if she can? If we leave early in the morning and come back late afternoon, it would work."

She paced away, her thoughts muddled at leaving her home and traveling to his. She wasn't sure she was ready to do that, but he seemed to think she could.

She returned shortly, stopping in the doorway, watching as he worked at the oilcloth, turning it over and over to try and figure it out.

"Rory?" He turned as he heard her voice, a smile on his face. "Lisa can be here by 6. Will that work?"

"It will. If we're away by 7 at the latest, we can have breakfast with my mom."

Leah was shaking her head. "Oh, I couldn't do that. She doesn't know me, not that well."

He walked towards her, his hands coming up to cup her shoulders. "It doesn't matter. She's been here. She will welcome you into her home gladly." He paused, seeking for words to reassure her. "She welcomes complete strangers in their home and makes them a friend. You are a friend. You are more than welcome in their home."

She finally agreed to do that, but he could tell she was still very uncertain. "Listen, if it stresses you that much, we can catch breakfast in a restaurant and then head for our offices."

"Is that where you need to go with that?" She pointed to the oilskin.

"It is. Reilly is really interested in old documents and has studied them. He may be able to sort this out. If not, he'll know who we can talk to. Mom will want to take a look at it as well, even though it's not a book."

"He would do that? I'm a stranger to him."

"It doesn't matter." Rory hesitated for a moment before he pulled her into a hug, waiting until she finally reached to hug him back. "He knows you're my friend. They all do. I can't emphasize that enough. Even for strangers, they do this. That's who we are. They would drop everything they were doing if they needed to and if I asked for help."

She sighed, the sigh drawn from deep within her. "I have never felt that of my friends. I know they will help, but there has been a hesitation there."

Rory hesitated before he spoke. "I don't think you have ever been told how much your family is respected and loved in this town. Have you?" He felt her head shaking. "You are, you know. When I've been down town, I am questioned as to how you are, do you need anything, what can they do to help you. You didn't know that?"

She leaned back as far as his arms would let her. "They wouldn't say that. They were angry with Gramps and Grams because they refused to give access to the beach and the bay."

"Not everyone. I was told about that. The persons responsible for that have left town."

She shoved at him until he released her and then turned and walked away. "I can't do this right now, Rory. I can't take that in. It's never been like that." She spun, storming back towards him. "And if they say different, what can I say? I know what Grams was told. I was there. So for them to ask that, I just…". Her words died away and he saw the tears sparkling on her cheeks before she turned and once more walked away from him.

He sighed. That went well, now didn't it, Lord? How do we reach out to her, to let her know that she is loved? I wish I knew how we could do that.

His vision caught sight of the oilskin map and he walked back over to it, carefully folding it again and then heading for his room. He hid it, knowing that if someone found it, they would never know exactly what it meant. And that would never do. A shudder of fear ran through him.

Lord, I am afraid, and I have no idea why. Please, dear Lord, guide us over the next few days. Help us to solve this quickly so that my lovely Leah can move on. Right now, she can't.

Leah moved almost silently through her day, her thoughts in a turmoil. What she had been told by Rory about the town's feelings towards her family didn't make sense. It's not how she remembered being treated.   She felt him shooting her questioning looks but she just moved away. How was she ever to spend the day away with him tomorrow when she felt like she did?

Early morning found Leah on her feet and in her kitchen, checking the lists she had left for her friend, Lisa, to follow. Lisa had already arrived and headed for the dining room, knowing what needed to be done. Leah sighed. This is not easy, Lord, letting someone else take over so I can leave for a day away. How long has that been? Years, I think, since I've taken a whole day just for me. Well, not actually just for me. Rory is pushing and I don't know how to tell him to slow down and back away. I really don't think he will, now will he, Lord? And do I want him to? I am so confused, dear Lord, that only You can straighten it all out.

She turned as she heard Rory's footsteps hesitate at the kitchen doorway and looked up at him. He smiled and reached out a hand.

"All set, my love?"

She shook her head. "Not really, but I guess I have no choice, now do I? Your family is expecting us and we can't disappoint them."   She reached for the knapsack she had packed, but Rory's hand was there, stopping her movement.

She didn't see Lisa hesitate before entering the room, moving silently to take the trays of foods she needed to put out. Leah looked up at Rory, a frown on her face.

"If you really don't want to go, we will cancel.   I will not force you to do anything against what you feel is right. Do you understand that?" When she just stood there, her eyes on him, he sighed. "Do you understand that, Leah? That no one is going to force you to get in my car and drive to my home town?"

She finally nodded.   "I do get that, Rory.   Let's go.   Lisa, we'll be back by teatime."   She moved rapidly past him, heading for the door.

Rory stared after her, his head turning slightly as Lisa approached.

"She's scared, Rory, and nervous. You're taking her to meet the rest of your family and she's never ever done that. She's never dated.   She always refused and she was asked numerous times. Even now, there are men interested in her and she just ignores them or doesn't respond."

"Thanks, Lisa, for picking up for her. She does need some time." He looked down at the petite woman beside him. "You're a good friend to her. God bless you."

He walked away, heading to find Leah. She was standing, arms folded around her abdomen, her eyes on the path heading towards the bay, a frown on her face.

"Leah? I meant it. We can cancel." Rory stood with one hand on the open car door, watching her intently.

"No, it's okay. I was just puzzling something out." She slid into the car, watching as he closed her door and then headed around to slid into the car himself. "I don't know about your habits, but can we pray before we leave? Dad and Gramps always did."

"We can do that. I was going to suggest that very thing." Heads bowed, Rory prayed for protection and safety during the day, not realizing how much those prayers would be needed.

Chapter 14

Leah watched as Rory headed back for her home town at the end of the day. Dusk was falling. She was later than she had wanted to be, but Lisa had assured her all was well and that she would stay over and work the next day for her as well. It had been too long since she had had a long talk with Leah and that was what she wanted. She stared out the window, her thoughts muddled, going back over the day.

Naomi had welcomed Leah with a tight hug and smiles, drawing the younger woman into her kitchen. Leah had stared, finally snapping her mouth closed, as the old-fashioned, yet modern kitchen. Naomi had laughed at her reaction, stating that was how everyone responded. Rory had kissed his mother, and then Leah, surprising her, before he headed off to find his brothers. It wasn't long before his sisters, Regan and Ryanne, had descended on the kitchen, taking stock of Leah before just enveloping her into their fun and antics. Naomi had watched for a while before she went to find her sons.

"Rory? What's going on? You hadn't planned to come back here, not yet." She stood, her hand on her son's shoulder.

"No, I didn't, Mom. Leah needed to get away. She doesn't show it, but this has really brought her down. I've seen her withdrawing more and more from her guests." He looked up at his mother, seeing her understanding on her face. "She's scared, too. I would say terrified."

Redmond spoke up. He was the elder of the children, who were all about one year apart. "What from?"

"If I knew, I'd deal with it." Rory rapidly spoke, sharing what had been happening, going back to the camera he found when he first saw her up until the text his father had shared.

"All that? Are you're just telling us now?" Reilly bit back his anger, not directing it at Rory or Leah but at whoever was responsible.

"I would have had I known more of what was going on. She still hasn't told me everything. Dad said he spoke with the police chief, whom he apparently knows. He didn't say what all he was told but it was enough for him to start making plans."

"Those plans? They're for you and Leah?" Redmond sat back, his eyes on his brother, speculation on his face. "Dad never said. Just asked me to draw up some plans."

"He did, did he? That doesn't surprise me." Rory reached for his briefcase, pulling out the oilcloth map. "Mom, you'll like this. Reilly, I found this behind a painting. I would say the painting was well over one hundred years old. I didn't bring it, just left it hanging on the wall where it's hung for years."

Reilly reached for the packet, hesitating for a moment, before he rose from the table they were seated and found gloves to put on. "Behind a painting? How on earth did you find that?"

Rory shrugged. "God, I guess. Dad had left and I was thinking of something, staring at this painting. It's of the bay near the B&B. Something just seemed different about it. When I took it down and we looked behind it, the paper backing was starting to come away. We found that." He held up a hand. "I was very careful handling it. We took still photos and Leah videotaped us opening it."

"Good. Now, let's see what we have." Reilly pored over the map, finally looking up at Rory. "This will take some time. Go, find your lady and show her around the property. She needs to know where the safety zones and hiding spots are, just in case. Dad was right. Looking at this and from what he's said and what you've said, someone is convinced she's hidden a treasure or one has been hidden there for years." He was back into his research before Rory could respond.

Naomi drew Rory aside, handing him a small box with a smile. "Here. It's time you had this. Go, find your lady love, my son." She hugged him and dropped a kiss on his cheek before she walked away, the door to the library closing softly after her.

Rory stood for a moment at the back door, watching Leah as she laughed and joked with her sisters, glad she was letting go of her fears for a bit. He had known his sisters would have that effect on her. Regan rose and came towards him, hugging him.

"Thanks for bringing your lady here, Rory. She's such a sweetheart. How'd you find her?"

Rory began to laugh, the sound causing Leah to raise her head and then she too began to laugh as she caught Regan's question.

"The old story of a gallant knight, wasn't it, Rory? I fell from a ladder and he just swept me off my feet." She blushed and began waving her hands as the other three laughed harder. "No! No! That's not what I meant to say! He caught me when I tumbled down from a ladder after he startled me!" She shook her head, tears of laughter sparkling in her eyes. "This is just making it worse, isn't it?"

"That it is." Regan finally took pity on her. "So, you fell from a ladder and he caught you. What were you doing up on a ladder anyway?"

"Trying to tidy up. Someone had tossed a bunch of stuff around and I needed to put it away." She paused, a frown on her face. "Rory, did you ever track down what was going on with that camera?"

He shook his head, movement to his left catching his attention. Redmond stood there, frowning. "It's okay, Redmond. Dad and I have gone over the entire place."

"You didn't say anything about that."

"I didn't? I thought I had." Rory shrugged as he slipped into a chair beside Leah. "Are you okay?" His voice was soft, hidden under the sounds of his siblings' chatter.

"I am. Thank you, Rory. You were right. I needed to get away. Don't tell your sisters, but they really are sweethearts."

He just grinned at that, reaching instead for a muffin from the basket in the centre of the patio table.

"Who baked these?" Leah had eaten one already and then reached for another one.

"Reilly!" The chorus surprised Leah.

"Reilly? Your brother?"

"I did. Want to make something of that?" Reilly's amused voice from behind her had her covering her face with her hands.

"They're good. I just wondered."

"Reilly likes to bake. He always had. We thought for sure he'd become a baker."

"Then I would no longer enjoy baking. It's a stress reliever for me." He sat, his eyes flickering between Rory and Leah. "Why?"

"Why what?" Leah had a good idea what he was asking.

"Why did you ask who baked them?" Elbows on the table, he watched her closely.

"Because I would buy them for my B&B. My guests would enjoy them."

"Then, we'll work something out. You're not that far away, and they do freeze." Reilly looked over her head at Rory, who narrowed his eyes. "I need to talk to you, Leah. Is now a good time, ladies?"

"As good as ever. We want to know what you were up to." Regan made a face at her brother, causing her other siblings to grin and Leah to stare, suddenly wishing she had had a brother or sister.

"You know what they say about curiosity and the cat, sis." He laughed, then sobered. "Your map, Leah? You've never ever seen it before?"

She shook her head, a thoughtful look on her face. "No, I don't think I do. It looks familiar, but then I grew up wandering the bay and the area. Why?"

"Because it's likely what whoever has been stalking you is after. It's very detailed for its time."

She stared at him, unconsciously reaching for Rory's hand, which tightened over hers. "What do you mean?"

"That it does suggest there is something buried somewhere on your property. Just where, I can't tell without seeing the actual land itself. Is there a day I can come by and do just that?"

Leah shrugged. "It doesn't really matter what day. Rory can show you the beach."

Reilly was shaking his head before she finished. "I know he can, but not like you. You know the history. You know that area. You can tell me about better than anyone, can't you?" He grinned at her, and she thought how much like Rory he was.

She finally searched Rory's face, seeing his acceptance of her and knowing that he would back whatever decision she made, whether he totally agreed with it or not. "I've talked to Lisa. She's staying over until tomorrow. Would that work?"

Reilly pulled out his phone and searched through his calendar. "I can make it work. I have an appointment I can switch." At a sound from Leah, he looked up, seeing distress on her face and he frowned, his eyes turning to Rory.

Rory nodded, his eyes going to Leah and then back to Reilly. "Reilly would not have offered to come tomorrow if he couldn't, my love. If he says he can, then he can."

Leah turned for a moment to study Rory and then turned back to Reilly, missing the looks on the faces of the other three Stuart siblings. They looked among themselves, small nods and hidden smiles shared. "Okay, then. I guess. It's a lighter day for bookings, so you can look around the empty rooms if you need to. I can't let you go into the occupied rooms. Not unless I have a really good reason to do that and I've cleared that with my guests. Right now, I would rather not do that."

"That's okay." Reilly leaned forward. "Tell me about Amy Townsend. Rory mentioned her, said she had been helping you, and then left abruptly."

"Amy? I don't know a lot about her. She talked a lot, but she said little about herself." Leah looked over at Rory, who nodded. "So I didn't learn a whole lot. I was sort of glad when she left. I was going to have to tell her I couldn't use her. Without more information on her, I just couldn't put her in a place of responsibility or let her go in and out of the guests' rooms."

"A wise decision." Reilly hesitated for a moment, his eyes on the hands he had now folded before he looked back up at her. "Amy Townsend was not your Amy Townsend. She borrowed that name. And she was not the age she wanted you to think. Our feeling is that she had been sent in by the ones searching your place and that she was responsible for the cameras and listening devices Dad and Rory found."

Leah nodded, a sad look fluttering across her face. "I really liked her, you know, and trusted her. But then she seemed to change and become more demanding as to where I would let her go. I'm sorry, Rory. I never told you that."

"That's okay, Leah. Don't fret yourself. I picked up something about her when I was speaking with her the last day or so she was there. Something was off. Her story was changing."

"That's it. That's what bothered me." Leah shoved back from the table and walked away, the siblings staring after her.

"Go after her, Rory." Ryanne pointed at Leah.

Rory shook his head. "Let her be, Ryanne. She needs some quiet time alone. She'll be back."

"And just how do you know that?" Ryanne moved to shove back her chair, but Redmond's hand on her arm stopped her.

"Rory knows her, Ryanne. Let her be. Rory's the one who will go after her if necessary." He caught her eye and shook his head. "Do you understand?"

She nodded, a sad look on her face. "Rory, just how bad is it for her?"

"What do you mean?" He watched his sister, reading her concern.

"I mean. She has no one of her own now. She's running a business where strangers come and go. Someone has been tracking her, more than likely from what you say. She's been threatened. What more can I ask?"

"There's all that, it's true. But she has a deep faith, Ry, deeper than most people have. Part of that is her training. Part is that she has had to lean on the only One she felt she could." He rose and walked away, heading after Leah.

"He's got it bad, doesn't he?" Regan's quiet comment stopped all movement of the other three.

"He does. And we say nothing." Redmond's eyes caught each of his siblings' eyes. "Do you understand? He doesn't need us interfering."

"He has enough right now trying to protect her and figure out what actually is going on. I agree. Let them sort it out by themselves." Reilly rose, heading back to the office, his mind already racing ahead on what he could find out.

Rory and Leah finally took their departure in the early evening, not feeling like they wanted the day to end. Rory headed for the place he now considered his home. He had had a long talk with his mother about life in general and about Leah. She had given him some advice when he asked. She was a mother who, even when she had an opinion and wanted to give advice, she waited to be asked, spending that time in prayer.

Rory reached for Leah's hand, linking their fingers before he raised her hand to his mouth and dropped a kiss on it. Her head turned abruptly, her eyes shadowed in the twilight as she searched his face. He knew she was watching him, but oncoming traffic demanded his attention. Sudden headlights beaming in his rearview mirror had him dropping her hand to grasp the wheel with both hands, alert to take evasive maneuvers if necessary. The large truck sped up behind them and then swerved, cutting back in sharply enough that Rory had to tap hard on the brakes.

"Just what was that all about?" Leah's voice was shaky.

"I have no idea. There are some people out there that shouldn't have a driver's license." He flickered a glance at her. "Are you okay?"

She nodded. "I am. Terrified, but I'm okay." She hesitated for a moment. "You need to tell me about your work, Rory. You've said bits and pieces."

"I haven't told you, have it?" He sighed, knowing she would think she had been set up. "Before I start, let me reiterate I came to your B&B for a rest, to get away from something that had happened about two weeks before I came there. My family runs an extraction service. By that I mean, we go into places and bring people out to safety. I have been to so many countries and helped bring out so many people. It is a dangerous work we do, Leah. Don't forget that. Dad has made sure we all have the training we need. It's usually just us guys that go in but sometimes, given the country or the circumstances, one of the girls will go in. Mom stays home and mans the home fires as she puts it. We do have more staff that just us. Two weeks before I came to the B&B, Ryanne and I went in to a friendly country. It doesn't matter which one. We were asked to find a teenage girl and bring her home to this country. When we tried to find her, we were stonewalled. We finally found her but it was too late. She had been given a drug but had overdosed on it. We escorted her body home." He stopped speaking, the emotions from those day overcoming him.

Leah's hand reached for his arm, squeezing gently. "I knew it had been bad, Rory, but not this bad. Will you continue? Have you had enough time?"

He shrugged as he slowed down to enter Angel's Bay before heading towards her home. "I have no idea, Leah. Right now, I just need time to decompress. Dad's letting me take the time I need. If I tell him I can't do this any more, then he's fine with that. He'll put me somewhere else in the company. He's done that before."

"He has?"

Rory nodded as he slowed to turn into the B&B driveway. "He has." He parked, then twisted in his seat, his eyes on her face. "I'm glad I came here. I would not have met you if I hadn't. We need to talk at some point, Leah. I really like this place."

Mischief sparkled on her face for a moment. "Only the place?" Then she sobered. "We need to, Rory. Something is happening."

Chapter 15

A grin on his face, Rory stood near the registration desk the next morning, listening to Reilly talk with Lisa. He's met his match, I think, Rory murmured to himself. He sensed Leah standing beside him and heard a low laugh from her.

"What's going on, Rory?" Leah's voice was quiet.

"Reilly is trying to sweet talk Lisa into letting him come back to your quarters, but she's not buying. Either that or she's decided he needs to be put in his place." Rory's chuckle was low as well.

Reilly finally looked up and saw Rory and Leah standing there. He shook his head as he walked towards them. "That's quite the guard dog you have there, Leah."

"Who? Lisa? She's really a sweet, calm person." Leah grinned at her friend. "Except when she's protecting me."

"Is that what you call that? She's good, you know. Rory, we may need to recruit her."

"Not a chance. I am very happy where I am." Lisa waved as she walked away, intent on cleaning the rooms.

Reilly watched her walk away, before he turned back to his brother, frowning as he saw Rory trying to hide his grin. He narrowed his eyes at him before glancing at Leah, to see her open smile.

"All right, you two. Fun's over. Let's get to work."

"In here then, Reilly." Leah led the way to her office. "Where do you want to start?"

"First, let me look at that painting. Then I want to walk to the bay. Is it far?"

"Not really, if we cut through the trees. Some say it's about five miles from here, but we can easily walk it on the path I use in about thirty minutes." Leah turned to go find the painting, to meet Rory returning with it.

"Here you go, Reilly. Now what?"

"Let me look it over. I'll need about thirty minutes, if I can."

Leah shrugged. "Okay, then. Come find me when you're done." She walked away, a sag to her shoulders.

Rory gave a growl. "Reilly, did you have to be so abrupt?"

Reilly looked up, surprised at the bite in his brother's words. "What do you mean?"

"She's hurting and wants to know what you're doing and why. You just shoved her aside. I won't have that. If that's how it's going to be, I'll find someone else to help us."

Reilly stared at his brother, shocked for a moment at the vehemence in Rory's words before he flushed. "I'm sorry, Rory. I was abrupt, wasn't I? Go find her. I'll explain what I'm doing to her so she knows."

Rory was away and tugging Leah back with him in short order. Reilly could hear her protesting and turned.

"I'm sorry, Leah. I didn't think. I'm so used to working for clients that aren't on site, I never thought you would want to hear what I'm doing."

"Well, I do!   And don't forget that! Ever!" She was angry and knew better, but she had been through so much in the last couple of years, she was worn out.

"I won't. I promise you that." Reilly waited until she nodded and her eyes found Rory, who smiled at her. "Okay. So, your painting? It's been here for years, you say?"

"It has.   It was given to my grandfather, my great-grandfather, something like that."   She watched as he scanned it and then reached for a magnifying glass. "What is that for?"

"I'm looking for any imperfections, bumps, whatever, that would lead me to think that there is something under this painting. It's of the bay?"

"I believe it is.   Have you found anything?"

"No, and I would have thought that I would have.   Do you know who the artist is?"

She shook her head. "No.   Grams never knew and if Gramps knew, he never said." She chewed at her lip and then shook her head again. "No, I don't remember anything ever being said. Not even Dad said anything about it. Mom never liked it for some reason. She felt evil in it."

Rory and Reilly shared a look before Rory spoke. "She did? Did she say why?"

She shook her head. "No, she just couldn't decide what it was. I've never really liked it but couldn't part with it, it's been in the family for so long."

Reilly stared at her for a moment before he reached for his briefcase. "In that case, can I take it apart?"

She shrugged. "Go for it. Now, if you'll excuse me, I have some work to do in the kitchen." She walked away, leaving the two men staring after her.

"What are you thinking you'll find, Reilly?" Rory finally spoke.

"I have no idea, Rory."

Reilly worked away for a while before he gave an exclamation. Rory rose from where he had been working and approached.

"What did you find?"

"This." Reilly held up a small key. "It was hidden in the frame. Now, I wonder what it fits."

"Let's see." Leah's voice had him turning towards her as she reached for the key. "I think I know what this opens." She spun, heading for the kitchen. "We've had a metal chest stuck away in the pantry for as long as I can remember. I had forgotten about it." She moved to step up on a ladder only to have Rory's hand stopping her and then he was climbing up, moving objects and boxes aside.

"Here, Reilly. Can you grab it? It's not heavy." Rory was back down, the ladder away, before Reilly had moved back to the office.

Rory stood, his arm around Leah, as they watched Reilly carefully work the lock, hearing it finally snick open.

Leah moved forward, eager to see what was inside. Reilly shot Rory a look and saw his nod.

"Leah, you open it." She stared up at him, her mouth slight open. "Go ahead. It's yours. You open it." Reilly gave her a gentle smile as he nodded towards the box.

"Are you sure?" She was hesitant, her eyes searching for Rory, finding him nodding as well before he moved to stand beside her, an arm going around her.

"Go ahead, my love. Let's see what's in it."

She drew in a deep breath and then raised the lid, her hand freezing on it as she did so, before her eyes raised to Rory.

"Rory? What is this?"

Reilly and Rory both leaned over to look.

"That's a small leather bag, my love. Can we take it out, Reilly?"

"Let's get some pictures first." He reached for the camera he had ready, snapping a number before he nodded. "Okay, let's get it out. Do you want to, Leah?"

She was shaking her head before he finished. "Absolutely not."

Rory gave a small smile and reached to extract the bag, laying in on papers Reilly had prepared. "Okay, Reilly. It's your show now."

He nodded. "Okay. This is an old bag, without a doubt. At least a hundred years old. I would say closer to one and hundred and fifty. That fits with your great-grandfather, Leah, I think." At her nod, he continued to examine the bag. "Okay, let's see what's inside it." He gently loosened the ties and dumped out the contents, standing back in awe.

"Reilly? What are those?" Leah poked at one of what she thought were rocks with a slim finger.

"They're uncut jewels by the looks of it, Leah. We would have no way of knowing if they were stolen or not. Not at this point." He shared a glance with Rory. "We'll document them and then put them somewhere safe."

"I have a safe we can put them in." She stood, staring at the small stones. "What is their value?"

"We would need a jeweller to look at them, but they are likely worth a lot." Reilly smiled. "You might not have to work another day in your life."

She shook her head. "Not that. I don't want them." She turned to find Rory tight beside her, his arm still around her. "Rory?"

"Let Reilly finish what he needs to do. Then, we'll put them away." Rory nodded at Reilly and then led Leah away.

Reilly watched them walk away and turned back to the jewels, awestruck at the find. Lord, this is in Your hands. She'll need more protection that Rory can give her. He reached for his phone to send his father a message and then pocketed it again. He needed to talk to the two of them first.

An hour later, he went searching for Rory, finding him out in the yard, staring at the huge tree behind the house.

"Rory?"

"Reilly? What now?" Rory was frustrated but was trying hard not to show it.

"Nothing more from the painting. Now, the map. Has Leah ever said anything about a lighthouse?"

"A lighthouse? There are remains there that she said was an old lighthouse. It had become decrepit and a bad storm took it down a couple of years ago. Why?"

"Because I need to see it." Reilly turned as he heard a voice calling to them.

"Rory? Reilly? If you want to go to the bay, we need to go now. There's a storm moving in and we only have a couple of hours before it hits."

"I'm ready to go. Do we need to take anything?" Reilly walked towards Leah, Rory at his side.

"I'll grab the knapsack, Leah, and catch up with you two." Rory headed for the kitchen, leaving Reilly staring after him for a moment.

'What's with Rory?"

"Whatever do you mean?" Leah headed for the path to the bay, knowing they were on a timeline.

"That. He never used to volunteer to fetch a knapsack or anything if one of the other of us are around."

"He didn't? Perhaps because you never let him have a chance. Isn't that the case?"

Reilly stopped dead in his tracks, his thoughts tumbling over themselves. "You hit the nail on the head, Leah. That's exactly what Redmond and I do. We take over things like that, not letting him have a chance. How did you know?"

She shrugged as she entered the trees. "I just did. I guess I've gotten a chance to read you and your family." She turned for a moment, assessing him and then looking beyond him to see Rory running towards them. "Let him pick up once in a while and do things you would usually do. It will do all of you good."

Rory handed Reilly the knapsack. "Go on ahead. Dad just called. I have to do something for him. I should be about thirty minutes or so, I hope. If I don't get there, make sure you head back in plenty of time." He reached to drop a kiss on Leah's cheek before he spun, heading back for the house.

Reilly's eyebrows raised at that as Leah stared after Rory, her hand to her cheek, lost in thoughts. Really shook his head. You have it bad, you two. He finally touched Leah's arm, causing her to jump.

"Leah? Lead the way, if you don't mind." He simply grinned at her as she blushed.

Their quiet conversation filtered through the air, joining with the songs of the birds, the frogs, and the insects. Sunlight flickered through the trees, playing across their faces. Leah finally stopped, her face raised to the sun before her vision caught the gathering clouds on the horizon.

"We don't have a lot of time, Reilly. It's moving in quicker than I thought. If we can do what you need to get done and head back soon, I'll be very happy."

"We should be able to. Where are the lighthouse ruins?"

She pointed. "Across the beach to the right. Come on. I used to play down here as a child."

He watched as she stood for a moment, hand on one of the stones from the ruins, before he dropped the knapsack and move to walk around. "It wasn't that big."

"They didn't need a big one. I guess, from what I've been told, the angle of the bay gave good vision to the light." She watched as he took multiple photos and then moved in closer to study the stones.

"This didn't come down on its own, Leah."

"It didn't? I always thought it did."

"No. I can see traces of an explosion near the base, in-between the cracks here. Someone wanted it down for a reason. If they set the explosion on a night with a huge storm, no one would have thought anything of it."

"You know, years ago, when I was about ten, I remember hearing what sounded like an explosion, but that was already down. I guess that wasn't it, was it?" She looked up as she felt the wind beginning to pick up. "Reilly, we need to go. Now!"

"What's that?" Reilly's attention was caught on something in the ruins and he ignored her voice, digging down and pulling out the object. He quickly dropped it into the knapsack, pulling out bottles of water for each of them. "Hey, that's windy."

"I know. Let's go. We need to be off this beach when the storm hits." A crack of thunder followed by a violent flash of lightning and the quickening of the winds echoed her concern.

Leah turned and ran for the trees, Reilly on her heels, head turned slightly to watch the ruins, before he reached and grabbed for her hand, pulling her faster. Once in the trees, their steps slowed. Leah looked back at the bay, seeing the anger of the waves as they struck at the shore, and covered where they had just been.

She pointed with her water bottle. "See that? There have been people pulled out into the bay and their bodies not recovered during storms."

"Really? I don't doubt that." Reilly took a swig of his water. "Rory never made it."

"No. I didn't think he would. Come on. Let's get going before the rain really starts." She set off at a rapid pace, Reilly on her heels, before she stopped, her head tilted as she listened. "Do you hear that?"

"Hear what?"

"That? It sounds like a little kitten. But what would a kitten be doing out here?" She turned towards the sound as Reilly's arm around her stopped her. "Reilly? Let me go."

"No, it may not be a kitten. It could be something sounding like a kitten to get you into the trees and then have you disappear."

"That doesn't happen in real life." She struggled against him, finally standing still. "Let me go! Now!"

"Not if you're heading in there!"

She stomped down on his sneaker-clad foot, causing his arms to loosen and she was free, heading for the sound.

"Leah! Don't." Reilly was on her heels, stopping as she bent to pick up a little gray tabby kitten. "You have it. Now come on." He gripped her arm in a tight clasp, pulling her from the area and back towards the B&B. "Never do that again."

"Excuse me? You don't order me around. I am not under your protection, in case you missed that." She broke free and ran ahead of him.

He stood for a moment, face dropped in frustration before he ran after her, seeing Rory walking rapidly towards them. Good, he thought. He can deal with her. Then, Lord, forgive me. She's right. She's not under my protection, even though I think she should be. I do need to ask her to forgive me.

He turned as he heard a noise, tumbling to the ground from a blow to the head. He didn't make a sound as he was dragged back into the trees, the knapsack forgotten on the ground.

Rory turned to look behind Leah. "Wasn't Reilly right behind you?"

She spun as well. "He was. He didn't like that I stopped and rescued this kitten. Now, where is he?" She ran back the way she had just come, ignoring Rory's voice to wait for him.

Disappearing from his view, she slid to a stop, her eyes on the knapsack, but not seeing Reilly. Now where is he, Lord? He has to be here. He can't have just disappeared like that. She set the kitten down on the knapsack and walked back towards the bay, not listening to Rory's voice calling to her to wait for him. A noise to her left had her spinning, a cry of terror rising from her throat that disappeared as a large meaty hand was clapped over her mouth and an arm surrounded her, pulling her from the trail and into the bush. She fought as hard as she could to get away but was unsuccessful. As she struggled, she sensed another man moving in and felt a prick on her arm. She soon drooped, her last conscious thought was that Rory stayed safe.

Rory stood in the middle of the trail and reached for the kitten, tucking it inside his shirt, and then the knapsack, not seeing either Leah or Reilly. He feared for the worst, that someone had taken them. He spun in a circle, not seeing anything, the rain that had started wiping away any evidence, if there had been much. He called for the two of them, but heard nothing but the heavy rain drops and the thunder and the wind. He finally had to leave, to run for the B&B and for help.

The police chief stood in the kitchen, listening as Rory explained what he thought had happened. He nodded, knowing that Riordan's son would be honest and concise.

"There was no sign?"

"No. The rain had picked up by that time." He pointed to the kitten, cuddled up in a basket. "Leah had that. They may have used the kitten to try and trap her."

"And took Reilly as well, perhaps thinking he was you. What were they doing down there?"

"Reilly wanted to look at the lighthouse ruins. It's part of an investigation he's running for Dad."

"And until your Dad says you can talk, you can't." The chief held up his hand as Rory went to speak. "It's okay, Rory. Your Dad and I talked. He let me know as much as he felt he could about Leah. I agree with him. She is in danger. This proves it. What else can you tell me?"

Rory quickly went through all that he felt he could. Some of it had to come from Leah, he felt. Lord, where are they? Only You know. Protect them. Keep them safe.

Rory turned as he felt a hand on his arm and hugged his mother. "Mom? What are you doing here?"

"The chief called. He felt you needed some of your family here." She smiled as he groaned. "All of us. Your Dad's on his way home. Ian was already there. Your Dad was planning on coming home this morning but was delayed. He said he'd be here late tonight."

"That's good. Now, we need to plan. Chief, where do you stand on a search?"

"We can't do much right now, not with this storm. It's forecast to last until late tonight. Naomi, is it? Riordan told me about his family. I am so glad to meet you. We'll need coffee, food, and paper and pen. Lisa? You're heading out, aren't you? Say nothing about this please."

"Not a chance, Chief. My lips are sealed. Call me if you need me. Mrs. Stuart, Leah said you were familiar with what she did. Can I let you know where things stand?"

"That you can." Naomi walked away from her family, praying in her heart for her son and for Leah, who she now knew was the love of Rory's life. He had shown that without realizing he had.

Ryanne rummaged through the kitchen, finding coffee, tea, and making sandwiches for them. "We need to eat, people. We can plan while we're eating."

Regan headed after her mother, knowing she wasn't needed in the kitchen, but would be in other areas of the house.

Redmond shoved his brother down into a chair and then sat beside him. "Go over everything from today, Rory. Everything."

He nodded, a sober and somber look on his face before he rose, heading over to pick up the kitten and cradle her close to him. He blinked rapidly for a moment, knowing that Leah would not have walked away from this tiny critter. Sitting back down, he looked around at his siblings still there.

"They went on ahead of me. Dad had called, asking me to research something he needed to know right away. I thought it would only take about thirty minutes. It took much longer. When I finally headed out, it had started to storm. I found Leah but not Reilly. When I asked where he was, she ran back towards where she had left him. By the time I got there, they were gone. There was no sign of them, not with the rain." He sighed, a troubled look crossing his face. "Redmond, I have to show you something later. Right now, it's not mine to share with everyone. It's Leah's."

Redmond nodded, knowing that Rory was breaking her confidence in his ability to keep a secret after careful consideration. "What do we need to do for the guests?"

Rory shot a look at the clock and rose abruptly. "They'll be in shortly for tea. Leah usually leaves it just about ready in the late morning. Ryanne, we'll need hot water. Redmond, the coffee urns needs to be filled and then plugged in on the buffet table. Regan, there are trays of sandwiches and vegetables in the fridge." He stopped, as he saw the smile on the chief's face and frowned.

The chief rose. "Walk me out, Rory, please."

Rory stood on the porch, hands jammed into his pockets. "What next, Chief? How do we find them?"

"I'll bring in a search team of a handler and dog. But with this heavy rain, it's doubtful the dog will pick up much. We'll need to do a visual search."

"My family can do that. It's what we do for a living."

"I know. That's why I'm staying back for now. But if we find evidence of foul play, I will have to step in and take over."

"We know that, Chief. It's how we operate. Once we need to step back, we do." He sighed, rolling his head from side to side to relieve his stress. "I just pray we find them and soon."

"Me too, son. Keep me updated." He handed Rory a card. "This is my private personal cell phone. Call me on it at any time. Do you understand?"

"I do. Please, Chief, pray for them."

"I have been since you called."

Rory watched as he drove away, then turned to face the door to the B&B, reluctant to enter, knowing Leah wasn't there and he had no idea where she was. Wherever she was, he prayed she was okay and that Reilly was as well.

Chapter 16

The next morning dawned clear and crisp, but the ground was still waterlogged. Rory stood on the back patio, contemplating the path to the trees, knowing he would have to wear his hard boots and not liking that. He had become accustomed to wearing his sneakers over the last few weeks.

Redmond stood beside him, raising a steaming mug of coffee to sip from. Neither man had slept much the night before, spending a lot of time in prayer as well as discussing the jewels that had been unearthed.

"Would they know about the jewels, do you think, Redmond?" Rory's voice was quiet, hardly breaking into the silence surrounding them.

Redmond shook his head. "Not if you and Dad have scoured the place like you said you did. There's always the off chance that you missed something, but I highly doubt that."

"Then, what are they after?"

Redmond shrugged as he heard his mother's footsteps coming up behind them. "I have no idea. Morning, Mom."

"You two are heading out shortly, aren't you? Regan goes with you, please. Ryanne stays here to work in the B&B. She volunteered to do that, knowing what this place means to Leah."

"We're just about ready to do. What time does Dad get in?" Riordan's flight in had been delayed the night before because of the storm.

"Ian said around 10 a.m. Let's hope he's right."

"He usually is. Tell Dad I left everything I could on the desk in the office for him. My laptop has the searches saved under a folder named Leah." Rory reached to kiss his mother's cheek before setting down his mug and reaching for his knapsack. "If we're not back by noon, send Dad and Ryanne after us." He walked away, leaving Redmond and Regan to reach for their own packs and then walk rapidly after him.

Naomi watched, her heart praying hard, Ryanne's arm coming around her.

"They'll find them, Mom."

"I know they will. I just don't know when or in what condition. Reilly would have been back if he had been able to and brought Leah or else sent her back for help." She sighed, her mother's heart deeply troubled before she turned with a smile on her face to Ryanne. "What do we have to do now, love?"

"Baking, I think. The guests are coming down for their breakfasts. I'll look after that if you want to get started in the kitchen. This is when we could use some of Reilly's baking."

"It is. You know, your father has to stop at the house. Send him a text to raid the freezer and bring some of the baking from there. It will help." She turned, reaching to brush away a tear or two of worry.

Ryanne watched her mother for a moment before she sent off the text and then headed for the dining room, mingling with the guests and thoroughly enjoying that aspect of the B&B. She finally headed for the utility cupboard and the cleaning supplies, taking stock of how organized Leah was. That is such a blessing, she thought. Cleaning supplies ready to use. Lists made as to what had to be done. Menus prepared for the three weeks ahead. I'm not that organized. I need to take lessons from her. Please, dear Lord, bring them back safely.

Rory's footsteps slowed as he approached where he had found the knapsack. He looked around. The chief had been right. Even under the trees, the heavy rain had washed away everything. He looked around, turning in a circle, Redmond and Regan watching him closely.

"Where do we start, Redmond?" Rory finally looked over at his brother.

"Let's head to the bay and then work our way backwards from there. We'll need to search the trees along the sides of the trail as well." He placed a flag in the ground. "This is about where you found the knapsack."

"About five feet ahead of that. There, right there."

Redmond straightened up from setting the flag in the correct place. "I suggest we search this area first, then head for the beach. Regan, you and Rory take that side. I'll take this one." Redmond stared at Regan until she nodded in understanding. Neither one of them wanted Rory on his own.

They searched thoroughly, but found no trace of the two. It was if they had vanished from the face of the earth. Rory and Redmond exchanged a glance before looking at Regan, seeing the fatigue on her face and the stress and worry they knew was reflected on theirs. Where were they, they all wondered?

Riordan caught up with them as they stood near the flag, discussing their next step. He hugged each of them, then asked for an update.

"How far back did you go into the trees? What did you find?"

His quick questions turned their thoughts back to where they had searched, each trying hard to remember what they had or had not seen.

Rory turned to the left side of the trail heading towards the bay. "You know, something is off in this area. There's an area that seems tamped down."

"Show me." Riordan followed closely as Rory headed about twenty feet back into the trees, carefully moving aside the branches in his way.

Riordan's hand on Rory's shoulder stopped his son before he reached the spot. "Is this what you are talking about?"

Rory nodded. "It is, Dad. I didn't have time to search it, but I would be almost certain a body lay there."

Riordan shot him a quick look and then crouched down close to the edge of the area, his keen eyes missing nothing. "I think you're correct there, son. I would suspect it was Reilly. The area is too long for Leah." He spun on his heels staring behind him before he rose and paced around to the other side, stopping when he reached it. "There are footsteps here that aren't washed away. They were protected somewhat. They're too heavy just to be one man. I suspect that Reilly was carried out this way." He looked up at a sound from Regan. "Regan, can you go back to the trail, love, and send in a message to the chief of police? We'll need him here now. There are definite signs of foul play." He rose, a thoughtful look on his face before he walked back around to where Redmond and Rory stood. "We'll go back as well, sons. We need to leave this area for the police to search and we don't want to contaminate it."

Rory stood for a moment, his eyes on the area. "Any sign, do you think, Dad, of Leah?"

"I can't tell. She may have been here. What about the other side of the trail?"

Redmond shook his head. "There wasn't any disturbance that I could see, other than animal. How many men do you think walked out that way?"

"Two or three at least. Two sets of tracks seem heavier than they should."

"That would mean they have Reilly and Leah and have taken them away. But to where?"

Rory was reluctant to leave the spot, feeling closer to Leah there, but he knew his father was right. He turned, his eyes catching sight of something. His exclamation stopped his brother and brought him back to his side.

"Rory? What's going on? Dad asked us to go back to the trail."

"I know, Redmond. But look. There's a kerchief in there. On that branch. I'm positive it's the one Leah had her hair tied back with yesterday. Those are the colours she loves."

Redmond studied his brother for a moment before he turned to bend over and look for the kerchief, finding it fallen on a broken branch. He frowned. "It looks as if there's been a struggle in there. Leah must have fought her attacker."

"She would, if she could. I was giving her training in self defense, putting in time when she had it. But it doesn't look as if it worked."

"We don't know why it didn't. She could have been knocked out, drugged, who knows what." Redmond's hand on his brother drew him away from the area and back to the trail, where he filled their father in on what Rory had found.

"You're sure it's hers?"   At Rory's nod, Riordan paced away, his hand rubbing at the back of his neck, his heart raised in prayer for his son and for Leah. He turned back, assessing Rory, knowing he would have to get him away from there and knowing it would be almost impossible. He knew that if it was Naomi, he would not leave, no matter what.

Rory walked down to the beach, his thoughts sober. He lifted his eyes to the horizon and frowned. There was a boat out there and he didn't think he had ever seen one there before. He pulled out his phone, snapping a picture, hoping one of the girls could work magic with it. He sent it on to Ryanne with that request.   He turned, searching for the pile of rocks that had been the lighthouse. He had uploaded the photos on Reilly's camera, but wasn't quite sure what Reilly was seeing. Only Reilly could tell them that. He paced around the pile, feeling the rocks, peeking into crevices, the flashlight on his phone providing light. He turned, leaning back against the pile when Redmond and Regan approached.

"Is this the lighthouse?"   Regan too walked around it.

"It is. I can't figure out what Reilly saw." Rory turned as Redmond gave an exclamation. "Redmond?"

"This is one of the areas he focused on. Do you see it?"

Rory shook his head as he too looked into the area. "Redmond, do you have a flashlight?" He took the one proffered to him and shone it around. "Oh, my!" He jerked back quickly, his face pale.

"Rory? What did you see?" Regan grabbed the light from and she too stared down into the crevice before she gave a cry, dropping the flashlight as she paled and then ran for the water, heaving and retching.

Redmond stared in astonishment at the two. "What did you two see?"

"Human bones." Rory drew in deep breaths, trying to control his stomach as well. "Human bones, Redmond."

"What?" Redmond too looked and then stepped back, his face pale as well. "We'll need the chief to see these as well." His phone out, he called for his father, whose surprised voice met his comment.

It wasn't long before the police chief and their father appeared, each looking into the crevice.

"Did you see this on any of Reilly's photos, Rory?" His father's quiet, somber voice broke into his thoughts.

"No, I don't know, Dad. They may be. I didn't take a good look at them." He was pale but he was determined to find out who it was. His heart cried out in prayer for answers.

"Not a problem. We'll take a closer look." He pulled out his phone. "Ryanne? Did you look through Reilly's photos? Did you see anything odd? You did. Which crevice? Okay, that's the one we're at. It shows the bones, does it? I see. You enhanced the photo. Good work. Save it. We'll be here for a while and then head your way." He listened for a moment. "No, I'm sorry, love. We haven't found them, but we're still looking."

The police chief strode back towards them. "I've called in more of my officers. We'll seal off this portion of the beach. You said you had photos?"

"We do. We'll turn over copies to you."

"Thanks, Riordan. That will help."

Rory stood watching for a while before he wandered away, along the beach, his eyes in constant motion as he sought to find Leah and his brother. Where are they, Lord? Are they safe? Please, dear Lord, bring them back to us quickly and well. He felt Regan's arm link with his and they walked on, step by step, towards a large pile of driftwood.

"This is odd, Rory. Why is this piled up like this?" Regan moved away from him, her hand running over the softness of the weathered and gray wood.

"It is odd but Leah says the locals will gather the driftwood like this all summer. Then, once September comes and with it the fall, they have a huge bonfire down here."

"Oh, I would like to see that. We need to come."

"We do, do we?" Rory moved around the wood, his eyes searching for any sign of the missing duo. "I just wish I knew where they were."

"Me, too, Rory." She watched her brother for a moment. "Rory, can I ask you something? And please don't think I'm prying. I don't want you mad at me."

"What would that be, that you need to ask?" He watched his sister's face, compassion on his own as she struggled with a decision.

"Leah? Is she the one? Is she the one you've been waiting for?" She waved her hands at him. "I'm sorry. I shouldn't have asked that."

Regan was a year older than Rory, but it hadn't mattered. These two siblings were closer to one another than to the other three. It was just how it had worked out.

"That's okay, Regan. I'm not sure. I'm praying it through. And I know Leah is. We've only had a brief couple of times to talk." He paused, his eyes on the sand where his toe was digging into it. "I really don't know."

"Now I know how to pray for you, Rory. That helps." She paused as she looked down and her face paled again. "Rory?"

"What is it?" He dragged his thoughts back to the present and walked over to join her. "What did you find?"

"This." She bent down and picked up a watch, turning it over. "It's Reilly's, Rory. See? The engraving Pops put on it when he graduated from college." Tears sparkled in her eyes and then on her cheeks as they spilled over.

"It is his. They did come this way. That boat!" Rory spun and raced back down the beach, stumbling at times in the sand, to stand, searching the waters. "There was a boat out there earlier. I sent a picture to Ryanne."

Riordan approached them, concern on his face. "Rory? Just what are you doing?"

When Rory didn't answer, just keep searching the bay, Riordan turned to his daughter. "Regan?"

"We found Reilly's watch, Dad. Down by the pile of driftwood." She threw herself at her father, feeling his arms around her, hugging her to him. "Where is he, Dad?"

"I don't know, love. Rory? What are you looking for out there?"

"There was a boat there, Dad, when I arrived here. It's gone. I sent a photo of it to Ryanne." He pulled out his phone, walking away to talk with his sister.

The police chief had approached, listening to the conversation. "You're sure it's his watch?"

Regan handed it to her father, who paled as he saw it and read the inscription on the back. "It is, Chief. Naomi's father gave it to him." He looked up. "Rory saw a boat out there, but that doesn't mean anything."

"No, but it might. Can he describe it?"

"Better than that. He took a picture of it for some reason."

The chief nodded, heading for Rory. "Rory? Exactly where did you find the watch?"

Rory led him back to the wood. "Right here. Regan picked it up." He turned in a circle. "There is nowhere here they could be hidden, is there?"

The chief turned to face the woods and then the hills banking the bay. "There are caves around here. I'll call in the search teams. We'll need something of theirs to use for scent."

"I can get something of Leah's. Reilly's?" Rory thought for a moment. "He usually carries extra clothes in his car. Let's pray he did this time."

"Good thoughts. Here. You and I are heading back to the B&B and get that for the teams. Rory?" When Rory turned to face him, the chief gave a smile. "We'll get them back. I promise. Leah's needed in this town, and I sense that you need her as well."

Rory shrugged, a shuttered look coming over his face. "I might. Why is everyone asking that?"

"Because they've seen you two together. You're two halves of a whole." A hand to the younger man's shoulder turned him to face the trail. "We'll take this one. It's a different one that we came on but it takes about the same length of time."

Rory froze, his eyes on the trail and then he turned to face the water. "They came this way, didn't they?"

The chief stopped, catching Rory's meaning. "I think you're right. Where you found the kerchief and the trampled area? It's about halfway between the two trails. The way we think they moved would have brought them out to this trail. I have men searching it for anything."

"Thank you." Rory was off at almost a run, leaving the chief to shake his head before he too walked rapidly forward, his eyes searching the area around him.

Chapter 17

Rory paced the living room of the B&B, waiting for his father to finish his phone call. It was the next day, and they were no closer to finding the missing duo than they had been the day before. He was frustrated and tired, not having slept the night before. He didn't think many of the others had.

They had tried to keep the news as low key as they could from the guests, simply stating that Leah had gone missing in the storm and they were searching for her. Most of the guests understood, but one couple had declared that they would not stay in a place where people went missing and had packed their bags and left. Riordan and Naomi had shared a look, Naomi had gathered her supplies, cleaned the room, and moved herself and her husband into it, paying the rate Leah would charge. They would not let her lose money just because she disappeared.

Regan and Redmond had searched the house over and over, Redmond finding hidden staircases and rooms. Rory had stared at him after the first two and then asked, just how many did he think there were? Redmond had simply grinned, shrugged his shoulders and moved on. Regan was in her glory. She enjoyed finding hidden objects and finding rooms and staircases just made her day.

Ryanne was subdued, her thoughts and prayers on everyone, even as she continued to run the B&B, taking time from that to search through the photos Reilly had taken. The bones had been removed from the pile of stones, the chief stating that the coroner felt they were at least thirty years old. He was now tasked with trying to track down who they were.

Riordan stood for a moment, his eyes on his son, before he shook his head and headed for the outdoors. The call he had received had been disturbing, to say the least, and he wanted to sort through his thoughts before he talked to Rory. It would be a conversation that would hurt him, Riordan knew, and that was just something he didn't want to rush into, without a lot of thought and prayer.

Rory tracked his father down an hour later. "Dad?"

Riordan turned, a smile on his face. He was at peace, working through what he needed to. "Rory? How are you, son?"

Rory shrugged. "I'm not sure, Dad. I am really not." He stood beside his father, hands jammed into his jeans pockets, shoulders hunched against the cool early morning air, not sure if he should be asking his father anything. "Dad? You disappeared."

"I know I did, son." He reached out a hand to Rory's upper arm and drew him to a bench under a spreading oak tree. "She has a nice place here. It's peaceful."

Rory snorted. "It is, Dad. I've been able to sort through what happened and make peace with myself that there wasn't anything we could have done to prevent that death. We just weren't asked in time."

"No, we weren't. That's part of the call I was on. Jeremy called, giving me an update on that." Riordan leaned back, his eyes sliding closed for a moment. He was beyond tired, beyond fatigued. Travelling overseas did that to him, and he had come to the conclusion he just couldn't do that any more. "He also had word on that Townsend woman."

"Who, the real one or the fake one?" Rory leaned forward, elbows on his knees as he buried his face in his hands.

"The real one. She's been dead for a number of years. Someone used her name and date of birth to obtain false documents. He's been able to track down the woman and she's been arrested. She's refusing to say why she was here or what she was after. We know for a fact she was after something. The authorities in her town are preparing to go in and search her home, once they have their warrants."

"That's good. How is she connected to all this?" Rory turned his head so he could watch his father.

"We're still working through that. But that text message that you got, it came from a phone registered to her real name. Not smart of her to do that."

"No, it wasn't." Rory heaved a huge sigh, and then yawned. "Sorry, Dad. I didn't sleep last night."

"We didn't think you did." Riordan looked up as Naomi approached, a tray in her hands. "Here's your Mom. With coffee, tea and breakfast by the looks of it." He rose, kissed his wife, and took the tray. "Rory, you need to eat. Leah would want you to."

Rory finally took the plate of eggs and toast and his cup of tea, sitting back, waiting as Naomi sat beside him, her own breakfast in her hands and then his father sat beside him. Riordan asked the blessing on their food, and then prayed for the missing two members of their family, asking for guidance to find them and for God to bring them home safely to them.

Rory stared at his food before his father nudged him. "Eat, son. We need to make plans. And if you don't eat, you won't have the strength to get through the day."

Rory nodded, weary beyond belief, but knowing his father was correct. "I know, Dad. It's just hard."

Riordan swallowed his mouthful of toast, casting a glance at his wife, who nodded. "Okay, then. You eat. I talk. Will that work?"

"Sure, I guess. What is it?"

"Jeremy has done some research for me, coupled with what Reilly had already found, and what Leah has told us. Angel's Bay was used for smuggling over one hundred years ago. Silks, alcohol, contraband, jewels, stolen artwork. About what you and Leah had talked about, I suspect. None of this has ever been recovered. There have been rumours that Leah's Great-grandfather and grandfather were involved, but the town people are adamant that they never were. With the rooms Redmond and Regan are finding, it does make it suspect that they were." Riordan held up a hand as Rory went to protest. "Let me finish, then we'll talk. There were rumours that Angel's Bay was also a way of escape for slaves and those wishing to start a new life elsewhere. That would explain the hidden rooms. Redmond also said, just before Jeremy called, that he had found a tunnel and that he and Regan were trying to find out where it ended. That was over an hour ago. He'll be back with what they found." He paused to sip at his tea, setting his plate on the ground, staring at its unfinished contents, knowing he would not be eating any more.

"What your Dad is trying to say, I think, Rory, is that there is a lot more to this house and her story than we know or that she even likely knows herself." Naomi's arm came around her son's shoulders.

"How could she not, Dad?"

"It's easy to have happen. Things are kept quiet and then the knowledge of them die away. I fear we're stirring up a hornet's nest doing this."

"But we have to find them. And this is the only way I can think that we can." Rory drew a deep breath. "Are they alive, Dad?"

"I believe they are. They want Leah alive to lead them to the treasure. I suspect they may think Reilly is you. You two look a lot alike."

They looked up as Redmond headed their way on a run. Riordan was on his feet, Rory and Naomi following.

"Redmond? What on earth?"

"Dad, you need to come with me. Now. Mom, we'll be back. No, we didn't find them, but we found something interesting. Regan has gone for the cameras." Redmond held up the crowbar he was holding. "We need this."

The three men headed away from Naomi on a run. She sighed, stooping to gather their breakfast dishes, her heart praying for her family. Ryanne met her with a question as to what was really going on. Naomi shrugged, stating they had found something and what did they need to do in the B&B. Ryanne stared at her for a moment and without comment, turned to head to clean the guests' rooms.

Rory stood for a moment in the tunnel, letting his eyes adjust. "What did you find. Regan?"

Excitement shivered from her in waves. "This. It's a shuttered room by the looks of it. No one has been around here for years."

Rory stared at her and then at the boards blocking the door. "I am almost afraid to have it opened up, after what we found on the beach."

"I know. I feel the same way, but I don't think we're going to find anything like that." She moved aside for Redmond.

"Wait, son." Riordan stopped his movements with the crowbar. "We pray first. Then, you can do your demolition."

Redmond's hands were shaking as he applied the crowbar to the first board and levered it to work the board free. The old, dry wood splintered under his onslaught and the boards and bits of wood were soon stacked to one side. Riordan moved in to take over, working the crowbar against the door, finally hearing a satisfying crack and the door slid open. He paused for a moment, his eyes straining to see what was behind the door before he reached for the light Regan held.

He shone it around the room, a frown on his face. "This is interesting."

"What is it, Dad?" Rory spoke for the three as they crowded close to him.

Riordan moved into the room, swiping at cobwebs and dust as he did so. "This must have been a room they hid people in. You can see remnants of a wooden bed, a table, chairs. Metal pots and pans. Tin cups and plates."

Rory stared around as well, before he moved towards the wall opposite the door. "Dad, this doesn't match the rest of the wall." He took the crowbar and pried at the wall, hearing a snap and the wall section moved. "What do we have here?"

Riordan and Redmond moved in behind him, Regan behind them. "What is it?"

"It's another tunnel." Rory moved ahead, not heeding his father's words to wait. "I can feel a breeze that's damp. Does it lead to the beach, do you think?" His feet picked up their pace as he walked forward, eyes searching for anything that would cause them harm and seeing nothing.

Regan studied what she could of the tunnel. "This was dug by hand."

"That it was. It's old." Riordan's hand rubbed at the dirt wall. "Whoever did it knew what they were doing."

Rory stood on the beach, the entrance to the tunnel hidden by a strand of trees and rocks. "Leah never said she found this and she does say she played here as a child."

"Her parents likely put limits where she could play. If you didn't know this was here, you wouldn't have found it." Redmond walked away a few yards. "It's near the lighthouse, too. That makes sense."

"It does. The lighthouse would make a good landmark for those coming ashore." Riordan turned back to the tunnel. "Let's head back and see what we can discover."

He waited as Regan and Redmond moved past him, Rory standing staring at the pile of rocks. "Rory?"

"Dad, something's different there. What is it?"

Riordan stood beside Rory, his eyes scanning the pile. "There. Right there. A metal box that wasn't there last night."

Rory moved to pick it up, scanning the area. "I don't see anything else. It's small, isn't it?"

"That it is. Take it with you and let's go." The two men disappeared from sight, not seeing the boat out in the bay nor the reflection from the binoculars someone was using to watch them.

Rory watched as his father carefully worked the lid of the small tin box and then leaned in to see what was in it. He paled as he saw the objects.

"Reilly's wallet? Leah's bracelet? Dad? What is going on?"

"They're letting us know they have them. We'll receive a ransom note shortly, I suspect." He looked up as Ryanne entered the room, a photo in her hand. "What do you have there?"

"I enlarged the photo of the boat, Dad. Here."

He took the photo, Rory watching over his shoulder. "Good. Do you recognize it, Rory?"

"No, I don't. But that doesn't mean much. It could be from around here. You would need to speak with the chief."

"And that I will do. Lock this away, will you? I'll be back." Riordan was gone, leaving them staring after him.

Rory walked away from his siblings, head down, thoughts a mess as he tried to sort through what he had learned or had not learned. He sighed, knowing there was something missing that they hadn't found yet. He paused at the back door, then headed for the back of the yard, towards the garden bed where he and Leah had found that package. He paused, his eyes on the sky, before looking down. He frowned. What was this, he thought? What is laying there? There wasn't anything earlier when he had walked the yard to try and wear himself out enough so he could sleep. Not that that had worked. He hadn't slept.

He reached for the envelope, turning it over and over in his hands, before he opened it. He read through it, not liking what he was reading before he stuffed it into his pocket. He would wait, he decided, to see what else happened. There is no way Leah would have written him a goodbye letter and then left her home. No one would ever convince him that she would. He frowned and nodded, a satisfied look on his face. It wasn't her handwriting, that much he knew. It was to throw them off, he decided, and that he wouldn't allow to happen.

Riordan found him a couple of hours later, just sitting on a bench, a mug of tea in his hand that had gone cold.

"Rory?   Your mom is looking for you."

"Is she?"   Rory looked up through bleary eyes. "I didn't know that."

"How long have you been out here?" Riordan sat beside and reached to take the cold mug of tea from him.

"I don't know.   An hour or more, I guess." He looked at his father. "What did you find out?"

"The boat belongs to one of the local men.   He fishes at the mouth of the bay every few days to provide for a local seafood restaurant.   We talked to him.   He didn't see anything."   Riordan sat back, feeling the warmth of the sun on his face.

"Now what, Dad?   Where do we search?"

"That's a good question. I don't know. They will contact us again. That's a given." He turned at a slight movement from Rory. "Rory, what aren't you saying?"

Rory sighed, pulling the envelope from his pocket, staring at his name written on it. "This. I found it a bit ago. It's a letter from Leah. Or so the signature says."

"But you think it's not?" Riordan reached for it, pulling out the letter and reading it. "This is bad, you know."

"I know. But it's not her. It's not her writing. It's not how she speaks or how she phrases things. That much I know."

"I see. We'll need to give this to the chief."

Rory reached for the envelope, tucking it back into his pocket. "And I will." He leaned back, his face turned to the sky. "Where are they? They have to be here somewhere."

"They're close. Of that, I'm certain. Just where, that's what we don't know."

"How much have Regan and Redmond discovered?"

"They're still digging into the history. Regan is thoroughly enjoying this. I think, when we get back to normal, I'll put her on research."

"She's been wanting that for a long time, Dad. Did you not know that?"

Riordan shook his head. "No, I didn't. She never said." He sighed. "I guess I don't know you kids as well as I thought. Just what do you want to do?"

"I don't want to travel, Dad. No more extractions for me. I just can't do it any more. I was burning out before. That last one finished me."

"I see. I have a feeling you'll be wanting to live in this town. That we can work around. Remote work is available. I just need to know which part of the business you want to work in. I know where you would fit, but it has to be your decision. Yours and Leah's." He sat quietly for a while, his thoughts turning to prayer.

"Dad? I'm not even sure what I want to do." Rory finally spoke.

"I know, son. I've been there."

"You have? Your whole life is this business." Rory turned astonished eyes to his father.

"No, no, it's not. Your mother and you five kids are. If I had to walk away from it to keep you safe or for whatever reason, I would do just that. Keep that in mind when making your decision." Riordan tapped his son's leg. "I mean that, son. Talk to Leah when she's back."

"Why does everyone say that?" Rory was frustrated and it showed.

"Because we saw you together and see how much you are a couple, whether you're at that point or not."

Chapter 18

Turning to her side, Leah rubbed at her face and then held onto her abdomen, the nausea causing her to rise rapidly and feel for the door to the bathroom. She stumbled through the door, the door swinging shut behind her as she dropped to her knees, retching. She finally slumped back again the wall behind her, her head dropping to her knees as she wrapped her arms around her legs. She waited for her stomach to settle somewhat, shivering with a sudden chill. She had no idea where she was or what she had eaten but she planned to avoid them in the future. She reached to shove her hair back from her face, staring at the tangled strands. Just what had she gone and done, she wondered. She hauled herself to her feet, staggered as she did so, holding onto the sink until she felt a bit stable. There was no mirror and for a moment she was glad of that. She turned on the tap to run the water as hot as she could, reaching for a damp cloth and staring at it, realizing she had done this before and not that long ago. She wrung out the cloth and wiped at her face, not feeling much better. Letting the water run cold, she rinsed out her mouth. She turned, still unsteady on her feet, her eyes blurry and reached for the door knob, opening the door and then dropping back down on the pallet she had been given.

She lay on her side, arms wrapped around herself as she tried to get warm, before she once more drifted off to sleep. She didn't hear the steps of the man who stood over her, waiting for her to move before he stepped around her and stood over Reilly, studying him as well.

Leah stirred once more hours later, her head clearer. Her eyes opened and she scrubbed at her face, feeling the dirt on it. She sighed. What had she gone and done now? She searched the room, not recognizing it, sitting up abruptly, fear running through her. Her hands clutched at her jeans and as she studied them, she frowned. Her bracelet was gone. Now where was it? She hurried searched through the blanket she had been laying on, her hands stilling as she saw the form laying across the room from her. She rose to her feet, cautiously approaching and then dropping to her knees, her hand reaching to touch Reilly's arm. She shook him and then shook him again when he didn't move. Her hands reached for his head, touching the bloody mark on his temple, and feeling him flinch. She was on her feet and to the bathroom, finding a cloth, dampening it and then back on her knees at his side, carefully wiping at the blood, a mask of concern on her face. What had happened to them? She couldn't remember. She stared down at her mud streaked, crumpled clothing and knew it was more than a day that she had lost. That they both had lost, she thought.

She sat back on her heels, not sure what she could do. She prayed, knowing that was all she could do. Determination on her face, she felt his arms and legs and then his chest and abdomen. She felt him flinch as she touched his ribs and his right arm. She could do nothing for him. She returned to the bathroom, searching for a glass and then returning to the room, spotting the bottle of water. She grabbed for it and headed his way, her walk stopping as she stared at the opened water bottle. She could vaguely remembering sipping from it and then losing consciousness. Drugs. That's what it was. She had been sedated, she decided. She turned, almost running for the bathroom, her stomach heaving once more as she stood, hand clenching the bottle, the other the sink. She dumped out the water and rinsed the bottle multiple times before she refilled it and headed back to Reilly, dropping to her knees, raising his head and helping him to sip from the bottle. Gently, she laid his head back down and then rose, pacing the room, searching for a way out, knowing that even if she found one, she would not walk away from him.

She finally sought her own pallet, laying so that she could watch Reilly, alert to any movement he might make. Lord, I need to get him out of here, but I have no idea how. She slept, not hearing the door open once more or the dirty work boots stop beside her. She didn't hear the noise of frustration that came from the man. He was angry, angry that she wasn't awake, angry that his henchman had given her too much of the sedative, angry that he hadn't been able to find the treasure in her house. He knew there was a treasure there.

He walked over to Reilly, nudging him roughly with his booted foot.   Reilly groaned and then lay still. The man was angry over that as well. They had hit Reilly twice, knocking him unconscious. He hadn't roused, not that he had been aware of.

He turned, his footsteps loud and shaking the wooden floor as he strode from the room, slamming the door behind him, the lock clicking in place after him. He searched for his men, and his words and curses flooded the air around them.

Leah roused again, realizing it was the next day, her eyes seeking for Reilly and seeing him laying still. She sighed, and then rose, her hands rubbing at her arms before she picked up her blanket and wrapped herself in it. She didn't see a window but knew hours had passed. She felt the chill and wondered at that. She walked closer to the walls, seeing what she had missed the night before. They were rock. That must mean they were either in a basement, underground or in a cave. There would be no way out except through the door. She tugged at the door, finding as she had known she would that it was locked.

She turned away, desperate to get away, her thoughts turning to prayer, pleading for release from that dungeon she and Reilly were in. She dropped to her knees beside him, feeling at his forehead, alarmed at the slight fever she felt. This wasn't what she wanted to find. She found a damp cool cloth and placed it on his head, having helped him sip from the water bottle. He needed medical attention and she couldn't get it for him.

She sat beside him, her legs straight out in front of her, blanket tucked around her, her head back on the wall. She slept, stirring only when she heard the door creak open and steps approach her. She blinked against the glare of the added light the man held, her hand going up to block it.

"Where is it?" The guttural voice sounded familiar but then she shrugged. She might know him but she might not.

"I have no idea what it is you want."

"The treasure, Leah. Where is the treasure?"

"What treasure? There is no treasure. There never has been." Leah blinked the tears from her eyes from the sudden blow across her face.

"There is. I have documents that say there is. So, where is it?" When she refused to answer, his anger grew and another blow across her face knocked her to the floor, her head thudding against the rock and she lay still. He stood over her, frustration and rage building. She was weak, he decided, unable to take any punishment. He strode away, knowing he would be back, and knowing that he could and would make her answer his demands.

She didn't hear the soft clicking of the lock hours later or the soft footsteps that approached. She didn't hear the quiet comments and exclamations. She didn't know she had been gently picked up in caring arms and carried from the dungeon. Neither did she know that Reilly had been gathered up as well and carried out after her, the men moving quietly and cautiously until they reached a vehicle, setting the two captives down gently on blankets and then the vehicle moving away quietly.

She didn't know that the man returned to the room, unlocking the door and then standing, dumbstruck that they were no longer there. The level of his rage escalated, and his minions scurried to escape it. They had all felt a touch of it at some point over the time of their employment with him but this time, the rage was more than any of them had ever seen.

Leah didn't feel the kind hands that assessed her and then started the IV that brought fluid back to her veins and her body. She didn't feel the gentleness that cleansed her face, or the soft voices that exclaimed at the bruising on her face.

She didn't hear the worry and concern as Reilly was assessed and an IV started for him as well. She didn't see the looks being shot back at them from the driver. She didn't hear the muted conversation around her or the muted phone call that was made, assuring someone they were safe and on their way home.

Chapter 19

Rory looked up from his book, seeing his father walking rapidly towards him. He stood, dropping his book on his chair, and walked across the room to meet his father, a frown on his face.

"Dad?"

"We have some word, Rory. Come with me. We're heading back to the office for a meeting." Riordan walked rapidly away from the house, heading for his vehicle, Rory at his side.

Two hours later, Rory looked up from his notes, a frown on his face. "How accurate is the tip, Dad?"

"Fairly accurate. Redmond is finishing up running the information we need." Riordan looked over at the door to the boardroom as it opened, and Redmond entered.

"Dad, I think I've found them. I have no idea who took them, but someone saw people being carried into a building and finally came forward to one of our people."

"Why us and not the police?" Riordan stared at his son before he shook his head. "Never mind. Where are they?"

"In the old jail building in Two Back Bay." Redmond send down his paperwork. "I looked into it. It was abandoned about twenty years ago. It has been kept up, with tours being taken of it. There are some areas that are off limits for those. The person who came to us said he thought that's where they would be. Apparently he has been through that building without anyone knowing that he had been. There's a dungeon in the basement. That's likely where they are."

"Okay, so now what? How do we get in?" Regan spoke up.

"Redmond, you've talked to the authorities about it?" Riordan shifted in his chair, reaching for the papers Redmond was handing around.

"I have. They're going to allow us in tonight. They said they've had reports of suspicious activity around there, but haven't investigated, putting it off to ghost stories and rumours. They didn't like it when I told them they should have and that if our people are in there, our lawyers would be speaking with them."

"It's what time now, 5?" Riordan looked around at his family. "So, let's get set and move it as soon as it's dark. Redmond, you have keys?"

"Oh, yeah, I have keys. I gave them no choice in the matter, stating that if Reilly and Leah are there and harmed, they would be facing a lawsuit. They quickly gave me a key, and agreed to stay away from there tonight. I've sent Jeremy to watch for now. He'll call if he sees anything. It's about thirty minutes from Angel's Bay."

"Good move. Now, what are our plans?"

Riordan listened as his family made their plans, excusing himself to call Naomi and let her know they might have found them. He heard her sobs on the other end of the phone and wanted to be there to hold her. He promised to bring them back to the B&B.

He turned as Rory approached and reached to hug his son.

"Do you think it's them, Dad? That we have found them?"

"I pray it is. We need to get them home. It's been a long three days for us. This is what we do best, Rory, extract people from danger. Now, what are the plans? Are they finalized?"

"They are. Redmond won't let me go in, says I am the driver. I don't like that."

"But you are the best at that, Rory. You know that."

Rory sighed. "I know, Dad. I just want in on the action inside."

Riordan gave a grin. "We all do, son. We all do. So who goes in?"

"You and Redmond. Regan will stay in the back of the van and be ready to treat them if they need that. Ryanne will be on guard outside as you go in."

"It has to be this way, Rory. You're too invested in Leah to go in."

"I know, Dad. I just wish I could. What time do we leave?"

"Now. We need to get there and get our plans in place. It's an isolated building, outside of town. I'm told the road is not well maintained." Redmond stood there, shrugging into his jacket.

"All right. Let's pray and then get on the road."

Two hours later, dusk was creeping in as Rory turned their van towards the old jail building, dousing the lights and letting the setting sun guide his path. He watched closely but didn't see anyone around. He searched for a place to park, finally coming to a stop where Ryanne pointed. Whispered commands were given and Ryanne, Redmond and Riordan slipped from the van and headed for the building, using hand signals as they moved forward.

Rory twisted in his seat, watchful as was Regan as she sat in the passenger's seat.

"They'll find them, Rory. Trust me on that." Regan's voice was low. Her supplies were ready if needed. She prayed they would not be but was well aware they more than likely would be needed.

"I know, Regan. This is just so hard."

She reached to squeeze his arm. "Dad will get them. Trust him."

He sighed. "I know they will. I just want to be in there."

"And so do I. But we're needed right here. These are our skills. Dad knows that and placed us where he wants us. He would not have agreed to Redmond's plans otherwise."

Rory nodded, his eyes searching the dark, praying that no one came until they were gone. He looked up as he heard a faint noise and saw Ryanne heading his way, the shapes of his father and brother behind her.

"There they are. Can you see if they have them, Regan?" Rory's hand was on the key in the ignition, ready to start the van and get them away from the area.

"They have." Regan was in the back of the van, the door sliding open quietly and helping to position first Leah and then Reilly on the pallets they had prepared. She had paramedic training, something her father had insisted one of their team do, above and beyond the basic first aid they all had.

Ryanne was in the front passenger seat, Redmond at Reilly's head, holding it steady and Riordan was beside Leah as quiet words echoed through the van. Riordan looked up, catching Rory's worried eyes.

"She's unconscious, son. We don't know why. Go on. Get us out of here. Head for Angel's Bay. The chief is expecting us."

Rory shot one more glance at first Leah and then Reilly, turned and keyed on the ignition, pulling away from the building and easing down the road as carefully as he could, keeping the lights off until he reached the main road and could pull out and away, heading back for Leah's town. He didn't see the luxury car they passed, heading back towards the jail, or see the occupants cast a casual glance at them.

Regan began her assessment of Leah, reaching to start an IV, feeling her body over for injury. "She's dehydrated, Dad. What you would expect if she hasn't had much in the last three days. She's had a few blows to the face. I can see the bruising. It's recent, almost as if it were today. Who does that?" She shook her head. "I know better than to ask that, having seen what we've seen."

Riordan reached to squeeze her shoulder. "That we have. She's okay as far as you can tell?"

"She is. Rory." She raised her voice a bit, causing her brother to shoot a glance back her. "She's okay, I think. We'll know more once we get her to the hospital." She handed her father the IV for him to hold. She gave her one more quick check, before she turned to Reilly.

She paused for a moment, blinking back the tears in her eyes before she reached for her stethoscope and listened to his chest, frowning. "He has some congestion, Dad. I don't like that. I'm glad we found them when we did." She listened once more to the raspiness in his lungs, not liking what she was hearing. She felt along his ribs and abdomen, feeling his flinches at she hit sore spots.

Her attention turned to his limbs, finding nothing that would concern her before she reached to touch his head. Reilly groaned, his head moving away from her hands. She frowned, asking Redmond to hold his head still for her. She bent over him, a sound coming from her as she gently touched the spot again.

"He's been hit here. I would say at least twice. With something other than a fist on one occasion." She sat back to reach for the saline solution she had ready and dampened a towel, wiping at the spot, her face hurting as her brother hurt. "He more than likely has a concussion, Dad." She looked over at her father.

"I'm sure he does. I'm also sure he likely won't remember much about what happened." Riordan peered through the windshield. "We won't be much longer."

"Good. They need more help than I can provide." Even as she spoke, Regan's hands were busy setting up an IV for Reilly as well, watching her brother closely before she turned her attention back to Leah.

Riordan had seen his daughter in action before, but not like this. She was totally dedicated to treating her brother and Leah, not letting her personal feelings interfere. He shook his head. Was she in the wrong profession, Lord? I never pressured any one of them to enter the family business. They all chose to do just that, but are their talents needed and useful somewhere else? Guide in this, dear Lord.

Rory slowed as he entered Angel's Bay and headed for the hospital. The chief was waiting for them, ready to whisk the two into the Emergency entrance through a back door. Regan almost ran to keep up with the stretchers, her father at her side as was Ryanne. Redmond waited for Rory to park before they walked towards the building.

"Rory?" Redmond's hand stopped him. "Wait a sec."

Rory stopped, turning to his brother, an eyebrow raised. "What is it?"

"Who's her next of kin? Do you know?"

Rory shook his head. "She had none. She asked me last week if I could be that. Why?"

Redmond drew a deep breath of relief. "That's good. Then you can be with her. What would have happened if you had said no?"

"I asked her that. She just shrugged, said she'd deal with it if and when it happened and walked away. I had to run after her to tell her I would." Rory paused, drawing in a breath of relief and sending up a prayer of thanks. "I'm glad she did. It was almost as if she knew something was going to happen."

"I think we've been expecting something. Only we thought it would be you and not Reilly." They walked towards the opening door, Ryanne peeking around to find them.

"Rory? The doctor wants to talk to you. Did you know you're her next of kin?"

Rory reached to hug his sister, then draped an arm around her shoulders as they walked towards the examination areas. "Thanks, sis. And yes I did. She did that last week."

"Are things that serious between you two?"

Rory shook his head. "I have no idea. We were talking one day and I asked her. She said she didn't have anyone she would ask. She's that private. She just walked away when I asked why."

"But she chose you?" Ryanne hugged her brother. "I knew you two were close."

"Leave it, Ryanne." A hint of warning was in her oldest brother's voice as he spoke. "Let them be." He looked around him, seeing officers in plain clothing milling around. Regan and their father stood outside one of the rooms, speaking with a nurse.

"She's in there, Rory. The nurse said for you to go right on in." Ryanne watched with compassion as Rory hesitated in the doorway and then entered, the door swishing closed behind him.

"I'm glad the hospital is old-fashioned enough to have rooms and not just curtains separating them." Redmond gave a grin at her comment.

"As I am. What have they said about Reilly?"

She shook her head. "I have no idea. Dad had just started to speak with the nurse when he sent me to find you two."

Rory had hesitated in the doorway to breathe a prayer before he entered the room, finding Leah resting on a stretcher, the IV running from a pole beside her. He walked forward, his hands reaching to grasp the bed rail as he studied her face, seeing the bruising Regan had mentioned. Raw anger flared within him and he knew if the assailant had been there, he would have been tempted to return the blows. It had to be more than one. His fingers came out to gently touch the bruising, his thumb rubbing at the gently. He watched as Leah stirred, her head moving away from his touch and then back into it.

Leah felt someone touching her face, this time in a gentle caressing manner. It can't be that monster, she thought. Her senses alert, she heard the faint click of equipment, quiet voices outside of her vision, and the smell of disinfectant she associate with the hospital. Hospital? There is no way we're free and in a hospital. At least not me. Maybe Reilly is.

She felt someone's hand gently take hers. It felt familiar, as if she should know the person. No, man, she thought. There had only been one man who had held her hand since her father and grandfather had.

She licked at dry lips, trying to form a word. Her head was lifted and a cup of cool water held to them. She swallowed and swallowed again, before a low laugh was heard and the cup was removed.

"You can have more later, my love."

She recognized the voice, trying to open her eyes. "Rory? Are you captive too?"

"No, my love. You're free. We found you and brought you home."

"Free?" She sighed. "I'm glad." Then her eyes flickered open and close. "Reilly? He's been hurt."

"He's here as well, my love. They're taking care of him too." He looked around, found a chair and drew it up beside her bed. "I'm waiting on the doctor to come in and see you."

"I don't want to see anyone. Take me home, please." A tear trickled down her cheek as she slept again.

Rory reached to gently swipe at the tear, knowing she would be angry with herself if she realized she had been crying. Lord, thank you. Heal them both please. He turned his head as he heard the door open and close. His father stood beside him, a hand on his shoulder.

"How is she?"

"She was awake, worried about Reilly. She thinks he's been hurt bad. And she wants to go home."

"No doubt she does. Likely in a day or so. We'll see what the doctor says." Riordan was quiet enough that Rory looked up at him, seeing the worry on his face.

"Dad? No. Not Reilly."

"It's okay, son. He's going for imaging. They think he may have a hairline fracture of the skull. He has been hit at least twice, they said."

"No! Who could be so cruel?"

"There are a lot of cruel people in the world, Rory. We both know that only too well. We'll see what the imaging shows and go from there. They'll keep him here for a few days at any rate. He's dehydrated too so they're working on that."

"The raspiness Regan heard?"

"They're worried about pneumonia, but they've started treatment." Riordan studied his son and then the young woman laying sleeping. "Your mother is on her way in. Ryanne and Regan will head back to the

B&B overnight and to work there tomorrow."

"Dad, they were to head out overseas tonight."

"I know, son. I've sent someone else. I would not send them when they're worried about you and your brother. You know that. It would not be safe for anyone involved."

"Thanks, Dad." His attention turned back to Leah and he reached for her hand, finding her fingers tightening on hers. "I don't know if I can do this any more."

"I know, son. Don't make any rash decisions. Pray long and hard about it. As I said, I can find another area of the business for you to work in. That is not a problem."

Rory finally drifted off to sleep, Leah's hand tight in his. He didn't see the woman who stopped in the doorway, holding the door open with one hand as she looked behind her and then at him. A sound of frustration came from her and she let the door close as she walked away, mingling with the crowd in her scrubs.

Chapter 20

Rory stood at his brother's bedside two days later, his eyes watching as Reilly stirred. They had dodged the bullet, the physician said, avoiding pneumonia, although another few hours in the dampness would have changed that. There had been good news with the imaging. No fracture, just a concussion. He would need rest for a while.

Reilly's eyes flickered open and he frowned as he looked around, finally settling his eyes on his brother.

"Rory?" His voice was rough and hoarse and he had to clear his throat. "A hospital? The last I remember is the B&B."

"You've had an adventure, Reilly. You don't remember anything."

"Nothing. I have a splitting headache. What happened?"

"You and Leah were kidnapped. Would you believe we found you in the dungeon of an old jail?"

"No, I wouldn't." Reilly studied his brother's face. "You're serious about that, aren't you?"

"I am. Someone took you and Leah captive, carried you away somehow to that place, and imprisoned you there. We went in two days ago and found you."

"Leah?"

"She's at home. Madder than I've ever seen her."

Reilly gave a low laugh and then groaned. "Don't make me laugh. When can I be sprung from this place?"

"Tomorrow, I think. Mom wants you to stay here in town. She's settled in with Leah."

"She has? That's good. When are you going to marry Leah?" Reilly dropped off to sleep, not hearing the exclamation of surprise from Rory.

Rory sat back, his eyes on his brother, his thoughts turned to prayer. Then, he rose and began to pace. He needed to leave soon. He had promised Leah he would be back by 3 and it was almost that now. He rose, standing staring down at his sleeping brother, seeing the bruising on his face and knowing just how close it had been to serious injury. He drew a deep breath, made a resolution within himself and then walked away, heading to find Leah and to see if she was ready for that talk they kept putting off.

He hugged his mother as she met him outside the B&B, a watering can in her hand. He knew she enjoyed gardening and the gardens here had won her heart. She would spend many hours here, he knew, if and when Leah and he could come to an understanding.

"How's Reilly?"

"He was awake, Mom. Go on. Head in to see him. I can take care of what needs to be done. The girls headed home, didn't they?"

"They did. So did Redmond. Your father went but is coming back late tonight." She studied him. "Rory? What's going on?"

"Right now, Mom, I'm not really sure."

"Don't make any decisions in haste. Pray, please, son."

He dropped a kiss on her cheek. "That's a given, Mom. It's how you raised us, isn't it?" He grinned as she swatted at him. "Where's Leah?"

"In the office, I think. She said she had to work on paperwork, that she had forms to submit and only she could do that."

"She does have forms and payments to submit. She's right. She's the only one right now who can do just that."

He searched for Leah, not finding her in her office, but seeing the finished stack of bills and envelopes on her desk. He finally found her in the sunroom, curled up on the love seat, a favourite spot of hers. He reached to stroke a hand down her head before he sat beside her, gathering her into his arms. She snuggled down, instead of resisting like she usually did. Her head on his shoulder, she sighed.

"Content, my love?"

"Right now, I would say yes. I missed you this morning." She twisted her head to look up at him. "You were at the hospital?"

He shook his head. "No, I walked to the beach to look around again. It's as if we're missing something there, and I have no idea what."

"I know what you mean. I've puzzled through what we're not seeing and not catching it. Rory, I think we need to pay a visit to the local historical society and look at some of the old documents. Maybe then we can think through what we're missing."

"We will, my love. Regan has found a wealth of information on line for us as well and saved it all to a folder. She's about worn out your printer."

"That's okay, it was old anyway. Did she say if she found anything interesting?"

"That she didn't say." He searched her face, seeing the shadows still in her eyes. "How are you really doing, my love?"

She sighed, her head going back to his shoulder and her hand tightening on his arm, liking the strength of his hold and wishing it would never end. "I'm hurting, Rory. I want this over. I hurt that Reilly was taken along with me. That shouldn't have happened."

"Reilly knew the risk when he came here. We all did. At least, we do now. Dad has spoken with the chief here. They are no further ahead identifying your kidnappers or the bones found in the crevice."

She shuddered. "To think I played around there as a child and never knew they were there." She reached a hand to swipe at tears on her face. "Why didn't I?"

"That's because the ground shifted in the last few years and some of the ruins moved, exposing that crevice. We not likely would have found them except we were looking for you."

She nodded, then stopped abruptly. "Oh, no! Not him!"

"Not who?"

"Jeff Langdon. He disappeared about thirty years ago and was never heard from. Dad used to chase him away from our beach."

"We'll pass that name on but I'm sure your chief is already looking into him." He rested his chin on the top of her head, feeling content as she did. "I thought I had lost you forever, Leah. My heart can't take that."

"I was so afraid for you, as well. I don't think I could have done as well as you did, had you been the one missing."

"So, where does that leave us?" Rory reached for the little box he had set down on the table and opened it. "This was Mom's. She had it given to her by her grandfather as a little girl. She has rings that have been given to her that she has earmarked for each of us."

Leah raised her head, to stare at the ruby in the ring. "Rory? It's beautiful. But what are you saying?" She twisted to look up at him.

"What am I saying? That I love you more than I thought I could love anyone. That I want to grow old with you at my side. You are what my family has described to me. Each and every one of them. You are the other half of my heart. Will you be mine forever?"

She looked up at him, reading his face, his heart in his eyes. She blinked back the tears, letting him read her heart as well. He reached to kiss her, his hand tightening on hers.   When he sat back, her head went down on his shoulder and she listened to the strong beat of his heart, knowing that it was hers and hers only. She watched as he slipped the ring on her finger. Just the right fit, she thought.

"How did your Mom know?"

"How did she know? I have no idea, other than God. He prepared this for you. You are the treasure in my life, the treasure I was seeking but not finding."

They sat for a while, before Leah spoke. "Rory? Where do we stand with the investigation?"

"It's at a standstill for now. They searched the dungeon you and Reilly were in but found no evidence. Any evidence that you were there was gone. Someone cleaned it out after we found you."

"You said something about a boat."

"I did. They found the owner. A local fisherman they said."

She nodded. "But what they didn't tell you, I would gather, is that he is an ex-con, re-homed here by his patrol officer." She heard his indrawn breath. "Rory?"

"What was he in prison for?"

She shrugged. "I can't remember, it's been that long. Something along the lines of break and enter, theft, impersonation, forgery. Why?"

"That's what we've been missing." He reached for his phone, quickly calling his father and asking that he research the fisherman. "I know, Dad. You should have been told that. What else has fallen between the cracks?"

"That I don't know." Riordan's voice was distracted. "Rory? Has Leah said anything else?"

"Like what?" Rory grinned as she shook her head at him, a smile on her face.

"I don't know. Like maybe she remembers something her family said about the treasure that your brother found. That she knows who it might be. Anything that would help us find the culprit."

"We'll work on a list of contacts and connections for you, Dad, and send it on to you. As to saying anything else, does Yes to my question count?" He clicked off his phone as he heard his father asking him just what he meant.

"That was mean, Rory." She was laughing openly at him, her whole face alight.

"I know. I'm just getting him back. He used to do that to us as kids, tell us something and then shut the door or walk away, coming back later to confirm whatever it was. It was never anything bad that he did that with." He hugged her, kissed her thoroughly again and then sighed. "I want to sit here forever with you, but duty calls." He rose and then held out a hand to pull her to her feet. "What have you to do now?"

"I don't know. Your mom has taken over running the B&B so well, I'm not needed." She caught the look on his face and waved her hands at him. "No, I don't mean it that way. She's enjoying it so much, I can't say no to her. I will miss her when she goes back home. I do need to go to town and do the shopping for groceries. And I have to stop by the post office."

"Then, that's what we shall do. Come on." He reached for her hand, stopped in the office for the letters, tucking them into a shirt pocket, and then walked hand in hand with her to the kitchen, where she found her list, seeing that Naomi had added to it with a question mark beside each item.

"Your mom is so careful not to offend, it's priceless."

"She's like that. She doesn't want to tread on your toes. I'm sure she has ideas that would help streamline your business, but unless you ask her, she will say nothing. It's your business, is what she'd say."

Leah looked up at him. "She would, wouldn't she? I need to sit down and talk with her. She asked earlier if I wanted an investor to come in. I told her I'd think about it. Who is the investor?"

"I would say Mom or Dad. They would invest and then just sit back and let you run the business, not commenting or advising unless you asked. They've done that before, for friends, for employees who wanted to leave and start their own business." He hesitated for a moment. "We need to talk, Leah, about where we go from here. I've told Dad I don't want to travel any more."

"I agree. That last one really took a lot from you." She slid into his car, waiting until he was behind the wheel and had started to drive away. "What will you do?"

"Dad will just put me into another department. I can work from here remotely or go in a couple of days a week. It's not that far a drive."

Neither saw the car that followed them, tight to their bumper, the driver watchful for a chance to overtake them, and not finding it. They didn't hear the curses emanating from him. Rory parked at the store and came around to help her, his eyes on the car as it slowly passed by them, his mind automatically memorizing the license plate, meaning to run it later.

Rory stood later in the office, his eyes on his phone, fear once more in his heart. His father had returned his text, warning him about the car. They both felt it was the man after Leah. Riordan had said he had more information to share with them and that he was on his way back to the B&B. Regan and Redmond were headed off to another country for meetings. Rory looked up, searching for Leah and then running through the house, seeking her. His mother looked up and pointed towards the patio. Rory hit the patio on a run, finding Leah sitting curled up in the swing, the little kitten nestled down in her arms. He slowed, his breathing ragged, waiting for his heart to slow before he approached her, dropping down beside her and kissing her, before reaching a finger to touch the kitten.

"How old would you say she is?"

"The vet thinks about ten weeks. I need to name her." She looked down at the kitten. "I think Kaylee. Don't you?"

"Kaylee sounds fine to me." He hugged her tighter, then spoke. "Dad called. He's tracked down the license plate."

"He has? Already?" When he didn't speak, she looked up at him, seeing the fear on his face. "Rory? You're doing God's job again."

He sighed. "I know I am. I am worried though. Dad wants to talk to us. He's on his way here." He listened to the sound of tires on the driveway and the familiar sound of a vehicle. "That would be him now, I suspect." He leaned back. "He'll find us when he wants to. Let's pretend he's not here and just enjoy the twilight together."

She shook her head at him. "Be serious, will you?"

"I am. I never thought I would be in love with the feisty little lady who took me on the first time I saw her."

"I did that, didn't I?" She turned her head as she listened to the night sounds. "It's always so peaceful out here. Grams used to come out here to pray, called it her prayer closet."

"You have wonderful memories. I just hope what you've gone through doesn't destroy them."

"They won't." She paused, a memory tickling at her mind. "You know, I vaguely remember Dad and Mom discussing his grandfather and how he made his money. Dad never knew. Mom had asked him one day how he thought he had made it. They didn't know I was in the other room and could hear them. He said he didn't know, but that smuggling had been rampant here in Angel's Bay. His own father had said that there had been rumours about Great-grandpa. None of us believed them."

"Really? Do you know of any more diaries, notes, etc, that are around?"

She shook her head. "I don't think so. I know Gramps burned a lot of old paperwork one day. He was angry about something. I can remember he and Grams arguing and they never had words, not that I ever heard. Do you think he got rid of something?"

Rory shrugged as he heard the back door open and saw his parents heading their way, a tray in his father's hands. "He might have. We'll look through the old books next, my love. Dad? You made good time."

"Traffic was good." Riordan studied the younger couple. "We need to talk, once again, you two, but it can wait until morning. A few hours won't change anything. Now tell us, how has your day been?"

Rory caught the twinkle of mischief in his father's eyes and shook his head. "We're not saying."

Naomi stared between the two men and began to laugh. "Your own words, quoted back at you."

Riordan roared with laughter. "Pay back time. I guess I do deserve that, don't I, my dear? Seriously, you cut me off, Rory. Just what have you two been up to?"

Rory stared at Leah, catching the slight nod of her head, before he reached for her hand, holding it up so they could see the ring. "I asked. She answered. A ring found a home."

Chapter 21

Looking for his father, Rory roamed the B&B and then headed outside, not finding him. He stood, hands on his hips, staring around. He searched the outbuildings next, not finding him there. He stood once more on the back patio, looking around before he shrugged. His father would find him when he wanted him. He headed back inside to the office, to his laptop and his research. He hadn't found out anything yet that he hadn't been told about Angel's Bay but he was certain something was out there, somewhere. He just had to find it. Lost in his research, he didn't see Leah stop for a moment in the doorway, a softened look on her face, before she moved towards him, her hand coming to rest on his shoulders.

He started and then looked up, a pleased smile on his face. "My love, what are you doing here? I thought you were cleaning."

"I'm all done. It's almost lunchtime. Have you found anything yet?"

He shoved his chair back and then wrapped his arms around her, pulling her down onto his knee and kissing her. "Not yet. There's something there, I know. Maybe I'm just not asking the right questions."

"And what would be the right questions to ask?" Leah stared at him, and then turned to the laptop. "Oh, I see. That's what you're working on. Wait. That's not the right name."

"Which one is wrong?"

"That one." She pointed. "That's not how you spell Gramps' name."

"It's not? Then how do you spell it?"

"He had an odd spelling for his first name. Most people spell it Rowan. His was spelt Rouwen." She quickly typed in the name and sat back, amazed at the sites that popped up. "Wow! All those?"

"All those. Now we just need to narrow them down." He typed for a moment and then watched as the screen flickered for a moment and then only a few sites popped up. He studied them, his finger pointing at one. "What's that?"

"What's what?" She peered at the screen. "Oh, that. Someone tried to sue him years ago, saying they were the owners of the property. They lost. Gramps had all the proper legal deeds."

"You didn't mention that."

"I didn't? I guess I just didn't think it was important. I should have. I'm sorry."

"No, don't be and don't apologize." Rory looked around as he heard footsteps and his father appeared in the doorway. He tightened his hold on Leah as she tried to stand. "It's okay." He whispered. "He won't mind, not one bit."

She stared at him, then peeked around him at Riordan, who stood, lost in thought, his eyes on the papers he held. "Are you sure?"

"I am." He kissed her before he raised his voice. "Dad? What do you have there?"

"Rory? You're in here. I've been looking for you. Leah, you're here too. Good." Riordan crossed to sit in a chair in front of the desk, his eyes not raising from his papers. "Where have you been?"

"Right here for the last couple of hours. I was looking for you earlier." Rory's quiet statement finally reached through to Riordan, who raised his eyes, his face thoughtful.

"I was researching and got involved. What did I want to talk to you about?"

Rory grinned as Leah gave a soft snicker. "That's what we would like to know. What did you want? You said last night you needed to talk to us."

"I did, didn't I? Sorry. There have been some things come up about one of our extraction that have caused some issues." He stared at the two for a moment, before he frowned. "But that's not what I wanted."

"Dad? Gather your thoughts, please." Rory grinned as his father shook a finger at him.

"All right. So. What have you come up with?"

"Other than I had the wrong spelling for Leah's grandfather's first name? Not a whole lot yet."

"What's that? The wrong spelling?" That caught at Riordan's attention and he set his papers aside. "Now, that's interesting. Have you discovered anything yet?"

"Not much. We had just gotten started when you came in."

Riordan nodded, his eyes on Leah. "Leah? What else can you tell us?"

"About what? I think you've all picked my brain until you have discovered everything I know. The only thing you haven't done is gone through all those books." She waved a hand at the bookshelves. "There are some there that might help."

Riordan cast a glance at them, then glanced back at Rory, seeing for the first time that he was holding Leah. He shook his head. "Let me reiterate. You two need to stay as safe as you can. That means staying close to here."

"That won't work, Dad. Neither one of us could take be restricted like that."

"That's what I thought you would say. So what do we do, then?"

"Live our lives." Leah slipped away from Rory. "I need to go check in some guests. Let me know what you decide."

Rory turned his head to watch her walk away before he spoke. "Now, you can talk, Dad. What is it?"

"Was I that obvious?" Riordan shook his head. "I must be losing my touch."

"No, you weren't. Leah suspected you were acting but she would never say."

"And just how do you know that?" Riordan waved his hand as Rory stared at him without saying a word. "Never mind. You two have connected in a way I don't see often." He sighed. "I fear for you two, for what you're facing. This isn't over."

"No, it's not." Rory searched through his papers on the desk, extracting one and handing it to his father. "Here. I found this on the desk this morning. I haven't shown it to Leah yet, but I have to."

Riordan reached for it, his eyes on his son for a moment before they dropped to the paper. "This was just left here? So someone had access to the B&B."

"They did. Leah won't let us put up security cameras, so anyone can come and go unnoticed. What do you make of that?"

"They're getting desperate, Rory. Leaving this threat, that she turns over the treasure or face dire consequences? We need to talk to the chief."

"She won't want you to. She doesn't trust him, Dad, but can't tell me why. I gather her parents never did."

"That's interesting. I haven't read him that way, although your mother has always had reservations about him."

"She has? She's usually right about those things."

"She is." Riordan stood, his eyes on Rory. "Your Mom and I are taking Reilly home today. He'll be laid up for a while."

"And you want me to come back to work." Rory tamped down the disappointment he felt, knowing this was his work.

"No, I don't. You're not ready, even if you do volunteer to come back. I can see that. Frankly, Rory, I'm not sure you'll ever be ready to go back to that line of work."

He nodded towards the laptop. "That's what you do best. That kind of research. Meeting prospective clients. Think about that. I'll move you to one of those spots if you want. Randy wants to train for extraction instead of where he is."

"He does? That's interesting. Sure, Dad. I'll pray it over and let you know." Rory watched his father walk away before he stood, heading for the shelves that held the old record books. His hands traced them, finally pulling one free and opening it. He was lost in the book before he had turned many pages, not seeing Leah standing in the doorway, a smile on her face, a tray in her hands.

Leah set the tray down, her eyes dropping to the letter as she read it. She glanced up in fear, to see Rory walking her way, still entranced in his book. She tamped down her fear, knowing that he had planned to talk to her but hadn't. What next, Lord? When will we be free of these people?

Rory looked up, his face lighting with a smile as he saw Leah before he frowned. "You saw the note? I'm sorry, Leah. I was going to talk to you but Dad appeared."

"He does that, doesn't he? Just appears." She walked into his embrace, feeling the strength he held her with and knowing that he would do everything he could to keep her safe.

"He does. He's looking into that letter. But tell me, while we eat, why you don't like the chief?"

She shrugged as she sat. "I have no idea. There has just been something about him I don't trust. Grams never did, and she knew him from when he was a baby. There was controversy when he took over as chief, but I can't remember what. I tried to find out the other day but there is nothing on line about that. We would have to talk to people and that would get back to him."

"Leave that with Dad. He'll look into it." He reached for her hand, his clasp warm and welcoming. "Now, my lady love, we do have plans to make."

She stared at him, finally catching the twinkle in his eye. "We do, do we? And what would those be?" She sighed. "Can we not? I'm sort of enjoying just being engaged for now."

"That we can do, my love, but at some point we will have to have that discussion."

"I know. I just wish this was all over." She pointed to the book he had set down. "What's with that?"

"Interesting reading. Did you know there are two Angel's Bays? Yours and one on the coast, about three hours from here."

"I knew that. What about it?"

"My question would be if they have the right Angel's Bay?"

She shrugged. "They seem to think they did. Do what you do best. Research it." She stood, gathering the remains of their lunch. "I'll be in the kitchen and then I have to work outdoors in the gardens for a bit, out front. They're looking a little ragged after the storm."

"And we have another storm moving in. Dad said he and Mom were heading home with Reilly today." He watched as her hands stilled. "They're not?"

"No. The doctors don't want him to travel that far. They'll bring him here."

Rory stood to envelope her in a hug. "Have I told you how much I love you?"

"You have, but I'll not stop you saying it again." She accepted his kiss and then moved away, intent on setting up the room for Reilly and then moving on with her list of duties.

Rory watched the doorway for a moment, a vision of her in a wedding dress standing there, before he shook his head and dove back into his research. He didn't hear his parents arrive with Reilly or his father take his leave to head home. He didn't see the darkness of the skies as more storms moved in or feel the tension and closeness in the area as thunder rumbled in the background and the odd flash of lightning flickered in the black clouds.

Chapter 22

A *loud* crack of thunder pulled Rory from his work and he looked up, startled, surprised to see how dull and dim the room was. At some point, he had reached over and turned on the desk light. He stood, stretching, his eyes going to his watch and he stopped. Five hours he had been working on his research. He needed to find his lady and his parents.

Following the sound of laughter, he stopped in the kitchen doorway, watching as his mother and Leah prepared the trays for the buffet table, light chatter and laughter between them. He smiled. He was glad his two ladies got along.

Naomi looked up. "There you are. Just in time to help us carry in the trays." She paused, looking at Leah and flushed. "I'm so sorry, Leah. Here I am taking over your business."

Leah grinned as she reached to hug Naomi. "If it means you telling your son to get busy and help, that is totally fine with me." She just continued to grin as Rory shook his head at them and then reached for trays.

She stood for a moment, watching as Rory and his mother worked away, knowing it was an accumulation of years of working together, but still appreciating it. She turned as she heard footsteps behind her and frowned.

"Reilly, you are not to be up."

"I can't stay in bed any longer, Leah. Any chance for a cup of coffee?"

She turned towards him, looped an arm with his and led him to the kitchen. "I'm not sure you're to have coffee."

"I really don't care. That's what I want." He knew he was pouting, felt ashamed and opened his mouth to apologize.

"Nope, no apologies. You're entitled to feel cheated out of coffee." She set a cup in front of him before she sat across the table from him. "How are you feeling?"

"Better, thank you. You're okay?" He studied her face for a moment. "Mom said you had some bruising on your face."

"I did. I talked back and I guess I shouldn't have."

He began to laugh, then stopped. "Please, don't make me laugh. It hurts. I can't see you talking back, ever."

She shook her head at him. "When do they let you go home?"

"The doctor said in a couple of days. I wish I could go now."

"I know what you mean. There's nothing like being sick and away from home."

He nodded, his eyes suddenly catching her hands as she played with her mug and he reached for her hand. "And what is this?"

She blushed, seeing the teasing look in his eye but also the caring. "Yes, your brother thought I needed it."

Reilly began to laugh. "He did, did he? I'm glad. You and he make a great couple." He turned his head as he heard footsteps coming their way. "Where does your mystery stand?"

"About there. We discovered you have been using the wrong spelling for my great-grandfather's name. Apparently there were two of them."

"There were? Now, that's interesting. Maybe that would explain it."

"Explain what?" Rory sat beside Leah, reaching to kiss her, causing her to blush once more before he draped an arm around her. "Reilly?"

"What? Oh, the two names." He was distracted, a thought running through his mind. "Leah, I don't know if we ever asked for the complete names and dates on your folks."

"Rory did and I gave them to him. I just didn't realize I hadn't spelt Great-grandpa's name for him." She studied his frown for a moment. "Now, what?"

"Now, what, what?"

She shook her head, biting back a smile, as Rory began to shake with suppressed laughter.

"What are you laughing at, Rory? This isn't funny. We're trying hard to solve this mystery and keep your lady safe." Reilly frowned at them both.

"You didn't hear what you said?"

Reilly paused, then shook his head. "No. I guess I didn't listen to myself. What did I say?"

Leah broke out into laughter, the peals of it echoing through the kitchen. Naomi looked up from the book she was reading in the sun room and smiled. Thank you, Lord, she murmured. She is just what we need in the family.

Rory began to laugh even harder. "I would say "what" is getting quite the workout." He took pity on Reilly, whose confused look was amusing. "Leah asked you now, what. You went now, what, what."

Reilly stared at them in shock. "I would never say that." He watched as they both nodded their heads. "I did? I must be losing it then." He grinned for a moment. "Now, Leah, Rory has researched your family. What has he discovered?"

"That I would like to know too. He hasn't said."

Rory sighed, knowing he wasn't really that much further ahead. "I need to take a look at the other Angel's Bay."

Reilly choked on his coffee. When he could speak, he asked, "There's another one? Where?"

"About three hours from here."

"And is there a house like this?" He watched as Leah shook her head.

"No, there isn't. Not that I remember." She paused, and then sighed. "I hear what you're thinking, Rory. You want to head there."

"Maybe. I'll see what I can find out on line first." He looked at his brother, seeing his paleness. "Reilly, come on. It's time you were horizontal again."

Reilly sighed, knowing his brother was right. "Thanks for the coffee, Leah." He rose, unsteady on his feet, before he headed for his bedroom.

Rory and Leah watched him walk away before Rory moved to envelope her in a hug. "Thanks, Leah."

"You're welcome for whatever it is you're thanking me for." She leaned back to look up at him. "Now where do we go from here?"

Chapter 23

Hearing footsteps coming towards her, Leah turned, a frown on her face. She should be alone in the house, everyone else busy elsewhere. She froze as she listened to the footsteps, hearing one set stumbling, others heavier. There were definitely more than one set. She rose from her desk, intent on heading for the outside door when Rory was shoved into the room, stumbling across the floor before his legs gave out and he fell to his knees. His hands hit the floor to balance himself and he stayed that way for a moment before raising himself to sit on his heels, his hands braced on his legs. She gave a small scream as she saw the blood trickling down his face and from his nose, her feet leading her towards him before she stopped, her eyes on the man in the doorway. Her head began to shake. It couldn't be. It wasn't him. But it was. Her hand went to her mouth to cover a deeper scream as one of the four men there moved towards her, his hand grabbing her arm and pulling her away from Rory.

She was slammed down into a chair, her eyes closing briefly at the pain she felt. She opened them to stare at the town veterinarian. Why was he here? Was he the one behind it after all? He was a distant cousin, she knew, not close at all. She had never liked him and had been glad she had no animals that she had to take to him.

"Leah, my dear." Dr. Todd Robins spoke to her, his voice silky but harsh. "You really do need to start cooperating."

"Never." She cringed as she felt the hands tighten on her shoulders to the point she knew she would have bruising there.

"But of course, you will. If you don't, he suffers more." The vet turned to look dispassionately at Rory before he nodded.

Rory's body slammed towards the floor again as he took a heavy blow to the back. He faintly heard Leah's voice raised in anger as she spoke rapidly, then his vision and hearing faded with the pain. He collapsed, to lie sprawled on the floor, his eyes closed, but his hearing clearing. He could hear Leah's voice as she spoke, anger in it, but fear underlying it. Please, Lord, take her to safety. I don't care about myself, he prayed.

Leah's hands were bound in front of her. The vet stood for a moment, his eyes on her, before he moved to strike her across the face. She realized then he had been the one who had taken Reilly and herself captive. She shook her head, regretting it at the pain that lanced through it, before she glared at him once more.

"Just exactly what is it you want?"

"You know exactly what it is. Your treasure. The treasure that should have come to my grandfather." He paced in front of her, agitation in his manner, his face full of hate and anger.

"There is no treasure. There never has been." She cringed back in her chair as he approached her once more.

He stood, his eyes on her face, before he shook his head. "Oh, but there is. My grandfather's diary says there it." He leaned towards her, a hand coming out to grasp a handful of hair, twisting it so her head turned with the pull. "And I will have it. Even if it is over your dead body."

Leah remained still, her eyes on Rory, watching as he moved slightly, prayers rising in her heart that he would make it through alive. She had no doubt that she wouldn't make it from the room alive and if she did, she wouldn't live long. She knew the cruelty that had been whispered about town, saw the fear and shame on the vet's wife's face and on the face of his children. She could only imagine how it had been to live in that household.

The vet continued to pace, his words coming fast and furious, to the point she tuned him out, her eyes on Rory before she heard a whisper of sound from the hallway. Cautiously she looked up, her eyes on the men's face and knowing they had not heard the sound. Please, Lord, don't let it be anyone who has come into stay. I know my business is closed and the sign is out but someone may have taken a chance. If it's Rory's family, take them away. Keep them safe.

Riordan's arm reached to wrap around Naomi and pull her back out of the B&B. He motioned to the other four who were approaching, soft laughter and conversation among them. They frowned for a moment and then went into work mode, knowing something was going on in the house that they need to be aware off.

"Dad? What's going on?" Redmond spoke for the group.

"Rory and Leah are hostages right now. I didn't go in far enough to see how or who. There have to be a least three of them, but I suspect more. I didn't hear anything from Rory, but Leah's fighting mad and talking back." He shot a look at Reilly who had groaned. "Reilly?"

"She's not talking back again, is she?"

"What do you mean?" Ryanne stared at her brother, not sure where he was going with his comment.

"That's what happened before, how she ended up with her face bruised. She talked back. She admitted to me she did and shouldn't have."

Naomi patted his arm. "We know, dear. She does have that in her to stand up for herself. She's had to." She looked at Riordan. "Now what?"

"We figure out how many there are and how to take them out so that we can get to Rory and Leah." He turned towards their van. "God must have led to us taking this today so we could travel together. Otherwise we would not have the equipment we need." He shoved open the van door on the side as Redmond reached for the back doors. They quickly suited up, taking their equipment. Regan hesitated as she reached to unlock the safe with their weapons in it, her eyes turning towards her father, who nodded.

"Unlock it, love. We'll need them. Pray we don't have to use them." He turned to Naomi, who had seated herself in the front passenger seat, popping open the glove compartment and reaching for the radio kept there. "You're set, my love?"

"I am." She looked up. "Go in and bring them out, darling."

He nodded, before he reached to encircle them all as much as he could with his arms, drawing them close to him, his head raised as he prayed. He knew their success was not just dependent on their strengths, their experience, their training. It depended on God, who would lead them into the fight and bring them through, no matter what happened.

He turned, silently pointing to each one and then to where he wanted them. Silent nods met his directions and they headed off.   Redmond stood beside his father.

"Where are they, Dad?"

"The office, which is good. We have access from outside to them. I have no idea if the doors are locked."

"I would say not likely. Leah doesn't lock them until night or dark. She likes to be able to go in and out without unlocking them."

"Pray that's what she's done today. I tried to talk her into locking them, but she just looked at me and then walked away." He shook his head as he remembered the look she had given him.

Redmond gave a low laugh.   "That would be Leah. She doesn't take directions very easily. Rory has his hands full."

"He does, but with his character, he can handle her. He's always been one who could talk us out of arguments."

"Or into something we shouldn't be doing."

"There's that."   They stopped at the edge of the front porch, disappearing from view as one of the man exited, intent on heading for the vehicle they had arrived in. They watched as he stopped to stare at the van, before he turned back quickly to head into the house once more.

Redmond's sudden tackle took the man by surprise and he was handcuffed and gagged before he could protest.   Hatred shone in his eyes towards them as they carried him to the garage and locked him into a small storage room.   Ryanne's head appeared briefly as she waved, four fingers in the air.

"There are four more.   That's not good."   Redmond's quiet voice caught his father's ear and he turned to stare at his son.

"Four?   We've handled more than that."

"I know, Dad. But it wasn't one of us that we were trying to extract, now was it?" Redmond's fear came through in his voice.

Riordan's hand rested briefly on his son's shoulder. "Steady, Redmond. We'll get them out. Never doubt that."

"I know, Dad. But will it be alive? I have no doubt that man would kill them if it served his purpose."

"He won't. Not yet. He needs Leah alive to find the treasure, and he'll use Rory to bring her to terms."

Redmond nodded as they quietly approached the office from the side, seeing Reilly at one of the doors, Ryanne at another.

"Where's Regan?" Redmond searched for his sister.

"I suspect she's made her way inside. She'll stay safe and hidden. That's her strength."

They pressed close to the doors, standing to the side, as they strained to hear the conversation inside. Riordan moved slightly to glance inside, stilling as he saw Rory sprawled unmoving on the floor and flinched as he saw a boot driven into his ribs, drawing a moan from him. He searched the room, finally seeing Leah seated, blood on her face from a split lip, her hair a tangled mess, but defiance coming through. Then he saw her demeanour change. Defeat was taking over, he saw, as she watched how Rory was treated.

Reilly moved to stand beside Riordan. "Dad, we need to get them out. She's giving up. That's not her."

"I know she is, but I need to assess this and plan." He watched. "Look, one of the other men are leaving. You two, head around and take him out."

Leah stared at the door, thinking she had seen movement, before she shook her head. It would be up to her, wouldn't it, Lord, to get them out of there, alive. Her eyes turned to Rory, her heart breaking at the sight of him. How do I get him out of here, alive? She prayed as she had not in years, her soul beseeching God for help.

The vet turned for a moment, thinking he heard a slight cry before he stepped to the doorway and stared down the hallway. Where were those two? It should not have taken either one of them that long to go to his car and bring back his pack with the supplies he had packed in it. He spun, his eyes on Leah, knowing she held the key to his fortune but she was denying it.

He stomped over to stand in front of her, bending over to grab her chin, and force her face up towards the ceiling. "Where is it, my dear? Tell me and I'll let you both go."

"No, you won't. Don't bother lying to me." She stared at him, compassion suddenly in her glance. "That's what you've been after all these years, isn't it?"

He shoved her back in her chair, marching away from her, circling Rory before his foot came back and he launched it with all his might into Rory's side, causing Rory to roll away from him and then lie still. He ignored her cries of anger to leave Rory alone and then her sobs of defeat.

The vet turned once more to face her, his face hard with anger before he once more approached her and yanked her to her feet, shoving her towards one of the doors to the yard. "We're taking a walk, my dear. Before we're back, you will tell me where the treasure is."

Leah stumbled as she was pushed towards the door, desperately trying to catch a glimpse of Rory, before the door was yanked open and she was shoved through, fighting to keep her footing as she stumbled. A hand over her mouth kept her from screaming and an arm around her swept her to one side and behind a male body.

The vet emerged, his eyes searching through the dimness for Leah. Not seeing her, he walked towards the yard, not seeing the men approaching him, or the two forms that had appeared in the office, weapons drawn and pointing towards his men standing there, shock on their faces, their hands dropping their own weapons before being raised to the ceiling. The weapons were kicked away quickly and the men handcuffed, forced to sit on the floor. Ryanne moved to the doorway, staying to one side as she watched her father and brother move after the vet before she stepped through and pulled Leah back inside, the door closed and locked, the curtains drawn. Leah ran to sink beside Rory, her cuffed hands reaching out to touch him, before Ryanne moved to unlock her cuffs, giving her a brief hug.

The vet turned as he heard footsteps behind him and saw the two shadows approaching through the rain that was becoming heavier. Realizing he had been found and had no chance, he ran for the back of the yard, desperate to reach the bay and the boat he had waiting for him. Thunder rang through the night and rain, loud in their ears, before a crack of lightning struck nearby, blinding them in its intensity. Riordan and Redmond covered their eyes, before they looked up, hearing a heavy thud and seeing one of the trees falling. They heard a cry from the vet and then silence. Reilly ran towards them, shock on his face.

"It got him?"

"What? The lightning?" Riordan turned to watch his son.

"No, the tree. He was under it when it went down."

Riordan stared at him, shock on his face, before he spun to look towards the tree, running towards it as Reilly's words sunk in. Reilly and Redmond followed. Circling the tree they could see nothing but the tree, a large old oak. They finally headed back for the house, Reilly around it to find his mother and the father and son for the door to the office.

The three women in the office spun as they heard the door rattle and then pounding on it. Ryanne gave a breath of relief as she recognized her father's voice and hurried to open the door, standing to one side as they entered, shaking off as much water as they could before they walked towards Leah and Rory. Riordan was on his knees, hands on his son, as Redmond hugged Leah to him, his strength flowing to her and helping her to stand.

"Are you okay, Leah?" His voice was quiet in her ear.

She nodded before she peeked up at him, seeing the grimness and sadness on his face. "The vet?"

He just shook his head. "I'm sorry, Leah. The lightning took down one of your trees. He was in the path of it."

She looked at him, horror on her face. "No! That can't be true. He had a boat waiting in the bay. Are you sure?"

"Reilly saw it happen."

"Is he sure?" When Redmond nodded, sobs broke from her and he turned her into his shoulder, his arms holding her tight even as he watched his father work on Rory.

Naomi gave a cry as she entered the office and she too dropped to her knees, working over him. Regan was there, her hands moving her parents aside as she worked on her brother, her face pale and worried.

In no time, the B&B and the yards outside swarmed with emergency personnel. The sounds of chainsaws competed with the sounds of thunder as the men worked to cut away the tree, trying to find the vet.

Rory and Leah were transported to the local hospital, Rory still unconscious. His sisters and his mother ran for their van, heading after the ambulance. Riordan stood for a moment, his eyes on the floor where Rory had lain, seeing the blood and knowing he could not let Leah clean it up. It would have to wait, though, until the B&B was released back to them. He had a friend with a cleaning business he would call in.

Redmond stood for a moment, then headed for the sunroom. Something in there had been bothering him all along and he had no idea what it was. He stood, his eyes on the walls before they raised to the ceiling. He ran for a ladder, coming back to set it up and climb to assess the beam running through the room. Reilly found him, puzzled as to his actions.

"Redmond? Just what are you doing?" He stood at the other side of the ladder, his eyes on his brother.

"Reilly? Can you find me a knife or a screwdriver or something? There is a slit here I want to open." He gave a quiet word of thanks as he took the knife his brother handed him. There was a small click and an opening appeared in the beam. He reached for the flashlight Reilly held out to him and then gave a low gasp. He turned shocked eyes to Reilly. "He was right."

"Who was right?"

"The vet. There really is a treasure." He was off the ladder and Reilly up on it, to stare in turn at the contents before he snapped the door closed and was down off the ladder and the ladder folded up.

"Don't say anything yet. We need to talk to Dad and then Leah and Rory. If we say something now, the investigators will take it."

“I know. I don’t like this, though.”

“We found it after the fact, you know. She has denied it all along. Let it lie. Dad can clear it with the chief, I’m sure.”

Chapter 24

A week later, Leah stood, mouth open, as Reilly and Redmond pulled journals and leather bags from the beam, Rory standing beside her, his arms tight around the love of his life.

"It's been there all along?" Leah was shocked.

"It has been. No one must have known, Leah." Riordan reached for one of the bags, turning it upside and emptying it of its contents. "These coins will bring a lot from coin collectors. We'll inventory it all for you. Ryanne will take care of that. Reilly will search through the journals. But I would say it's yours."

"I don't want it." Leah backed away from the desk, Rory watching her closely before he moved to draw her into his arms once more.

"It's okay, Leah. Let them take it with them. They'll lock it up and keep it for you. We can't do anything with it right now anyway, not until the investigation is finished. The chief said another week or two. They'll work on what they need to. You don't have to make a decision any time soon."

Leah searched his face, seeing his love for her and his confidence in her decision, knowing that whatever she decided, he would back her. "We'll decide together." She turned to Rory's family. "Thank you all, so much. I am so sorry I dragged you all into this."

"You didn't drag us into anything." Naomi approached her, hugging her to her. "You're part of our family, you know. This is what our family does."

"But I wasn't. Not at the beginning. It's gone on for so long." She wiped at her face, ashamed of her tears, knowing she needed time to heal.

"It has, and you are drained. Let yourself grieve, Leah. Take the time you need. If you feel you need to get away, let us help you. We'll take over here for you if that's what you need. If not, then talk to Rory, talk to me, talk to any one of us."

She nodded as she moved back into Rory's arms. His chin rested on the top of her head and his eyes closed in prayer. He waited as his family packed up and then left, quiet good byes said, before he drew her to the outdoors and their favourite bench.

They sat, the early afternoon sun playing across their faces, the sounds of nature in their ears. The fallen tree had been completely removed, but the scars in the ground were still there. Rory had found someone to come in and repair it, starting on the next day.

Leah finally spoke, her eyes on her ring. "If you want to take your ring back, Rory, I understand."

"And why would I do that?" He sighed, knowing why she was asking. "I love you too much to do that, Leah. If you'll keep it, I want to marry you and soon. You are my life, my heart, my greatest love next to God. I can't imagine life without you in it." He felt for her ring, studying the ruby. "You are my Proverbs 31 lady. You do know that, don't you?"

She nodded after a length of time. "I do. I do love you, Rory, so much so that if I need to let you go, I would." Her head turned so she could watch his face. "Where do we go from here? Your work is an hour away and mine is here."

He kissed her, stilling her questions. When he spoke, it was in a quiet voice. "Dad and I have talked. I'm not going out into the field any more. That's a given. He's setting up a new section of the business, dealing with lost treasures. He's dedicating that to you, you know. I'll be the one doing the research and initial queries on that. I can work from here most days."

She sighed. "Your father is so wonderful. He and mine would have gotten along great." She reached for the kitten, who had jumped to her knee, and cradled her close to her.

"I'm sure they would have. Have you thought anymore about hiring staff? You're busy enough that you need to."

"I have. Lisa wanted to work here but she loves her job at the school. I'm putting out feelers."

"What happened, Leah, is not your fault."

"I know. I just wish the treasure had never been left here. Gramps must not have known about it or he would have used it for good. That's what I would like to do, use it for good, for scholarships, whatever. Once we know the value, we'll make that decision."

"Some of it is unique enough to be in museums, you know."

She sighed again. "I know and if we do that, then the treasure seekers return and I don't want that. The vet was just so desperate to get his hands on it. He wanted to move out of the country and needed the money to live on. I feel for his wife and family."

"I know you do. It's best that he's not facing trial. It would be really difficult for them to go through that." He paused. "Mom and Dad are working with them, finding another town for them to live in."

"Your family is so special. To think a professional like that caused all this grief. He's the one, isn't he, who planted all those cameras and microphones or whatever."

"He is. He thought you knew about the treasure and that's how he would find out about it."

"Rory, those bones? Who did they belong to?"

"Oh, those. I had forgotten about them. They belonged to the vet's brother. He killed him in a fit of rage, apparently, and stuffed his body in there, covering it with the stones. The storms over time eroded the area and moved the stones."

"And how did you find that out?"

"His wife. She saw it, he threatened to kill their family if she told."

"How horrible! God protected us from him, didn't he?"

"That he did." Rory tightened his hold on her and reached to kiss her again before he whispered to her. "I love you. Let's set our wedding date."

She smiled, a hand to his cheek. "Is yesterday soon enough?"

He laughed and kissed her again. "Today works just fine. How soon can you be ready?"

She laughed. "Give us a couple of weeks. We have to plan this, you know."

They turned as a flash of light caught their eyes and they saw the setting sun sending out its rays. They sat, content to be with one another, happy that their adventure was over and that their live together would soon be starting.

Thank you for choosing to read Rory and Leah's story. As always, the characters have driven the plot line and the adventures they happened upon. I might have a plan in mind, but it gets tossed out within a few pages. They never like what I want to have happened.

Where is your treasure? In this story, an evil man was after an earthly treasure, not caring whom he hurt or what lives he destroyed. That happens when we focus on an earthly treasure. If your treasure is in God and heaven, then nothing can take that from you. God has promised that He will keep you safe. Jesus said that where your treasure is, that's where your heart will be. I pray that your heart is in heaven. Earthly treasures never last or satisfy. Unless that treasure in earth is in your heart and shows to those around you in your compassion, caring, and love.

We all face storms in life, some small, some huge. At times, we feel like we're right in the midst of one, at times like we're in the eye of a tornado. I've been through a tornado and know the fear that brings, how a storm can change your life. Storms cause us to re-evaluate what we have and what we cherish.

As I was writing this for the Camp Nanowrimo challenge, I had to make a decision about a young cat of mine. Ceilidh was only three, a rescue kitty a friend saved from a highway and I took in. She became very ill and with her illness, it would have been fatal. I had to choose to let her go. She was one of my treasures, that I lost but I still have my memories of her. Of course, given that, a little gray tabby girl had to find her way in the book, also named Kaylee.

Another challenge has been the sickness of my oldest of my three Shelties, Emma, who has been diagnosed with pancreatitis at this time. I love this girl, she and I have been through so much together. She has been through so much with me.

Earthly treasures come in many forms and shapes. Some we get to keep for our lifetime. Others we only have for a short time. God is there in all of this. My faith in him is the only thing that has gotten me through this.

God bless each one of you. Choose your treasures wisely.

Ronna